OUT OF THE WOODS

T.J. Land

There's a corpse in the mushroom patch.

Ruth isn't bothered; she collects dead things in jars under her bed. Her best friend, Hermana, is very upset, but only because the mushroom patch the corpse is lying in happens to be *theirs*, and the woods in which it decided to die happen to be *their* woods. Growing up shunned by the proper folk who live down in the valley, the two odd young women take a hard view of anyone who invades their quiet, wild world.

Their hopes that the problem will take care of itself fade when the corpse doesn't decay. Worse, when they try to bury it they find it's too heavy to lift into the grave; far heavier than a human should be. And when they try to burn it, its skin won't catch light. But soon the corpse's invulnerability and strangely pointy ears are the least of their worries. A fungus has begun to stain the ground around it, killing weeds and mushrooms, then trees and animals. When it reaches the river, people start falling ill.

As their home sickens and rots around them, the girls search for a way to dispose of the cursed corpse. At the same time, Hermana searches for a way to confess her feelings to Ruth, before her best friend is stolen away from her by the handsome nobleman who lives nearby.

This is a work of fiction. All characters, places and events are from the author's imagination and should not be confused with fact. Any resemblance to persons, living or dead, events or places is purely coincidental.

Copyright 2016 by T.J. Land

Published by
NineStar Press
SunFire Press Imprint
PO Box 91792
Albuquerque, New Mexico, 87199
www.ninestarpress.com

Print ISBN #978-1-945952-28-9
Cover by Natasha Snow
Edited by Raevyn

Dedication

To Kenny, Jess, and Étoile.

Acknowledgements

Many thanks to Raevyn, who rocks.

Chapter One

Ruth was the faster runner, with her long legs and whip-thin frame, while Hermana was the better climber, sure-footed as a goat, with short, strong fingers that could cling like grim death. They raced each other to the mushroom patch, up the steep slope and through the trees, and Hermana arrived to find her best friend performing a cartwheel through a cluster of dead leaves, the late afternoon sunlight flashing through her long black hair.

"Show-off," Hermana said, getting her breath back and rubbing the ache from her calves.

"Jealous bitch," Ruth returned amiably. She scampered up to a pale, moss-covered boulder they'd nicknamed the Cod, because it had a bit that looked like a fin, and Hermana had once scratched in a fish eye and two thin lines representing gills. She pulled Hermana up by the arm, and they hopped across the Cod's spine and down its tail into a moist, soft patch of dirt below.

Shielded from sunlight most hours of the day by the Cod and surrounded on all sides by drooping firs and slender ash trees, the next ten square metres of bare earth were lousy with mushrooms.

"Hello," Ruth said to them. She did twee shit like that sometimes. "How're we all? Keeping busy? T'rific, keep up the good work."

The mushrooms were their excuse for taking several hours every week—every day, if the weather was good enough—away from their chores. They always went home with two handfuls each, and usually they found berries as well or, if they got lucky, eggs. Hermana's grandmother made pastries stuffed with them, and Ruth threw them into stews for her brother when he came back from working in the village.

It could have easily been different, Hermana reminded herself whenever she was feeling sour, for though she'd never gone to church,

3

her grandmother had taught her to count her blessings. If she and Ruth had been born on one of the farms in the valley or had had baby siblings who needed taking care of, there'd have been a lot more for them to do. If they had grown up in the village, God forbid, they would have had to worry about getting the money together to afford ribbons and dresses and stockings, because you couldn't go about shoeless and loose haired when you crested seventeen in the village. At seventeen, you became a woman.

Hermana snuck a glance at Ruth. Like Hermana, she'd turned seventeen a few months ago, although they both still wore the same ragged clothing they'd worn as children. Ruth's shirt in particular was too small for her, a fact Hermana had noticed for the first time only last week. It left a band of skin just above her navel exposed, and there was an unpatched hole through which Hermana could see the edge of her left breast.

Ruth looks like a woman, she thought. Unlike herself. When she tied her hair back, she could pass for a boy. Not a bad-looking boy, granted; a damn sight better than a chinless wonders they had down in the village.

"What's wrong?" she asked, for Ruth had stopped short, sniffing the air like a fox scenting a dog. Hermana followed her example and wrinkled her nose.

"Something's dead," Ruth announced. "Maybe a day, day and a half."

In all the years they'd come here, their feet had never worn down a path through the shaded glade. Ruth took a different route through, every time, sometimes skirting round the edges, sometimes moving in a zigzag, and Hermana always followed in her footsteps. Apart from the hollowed tree trunk where Ruth had carved a picture of a spider and Hermana had carved her name, anyone would think it hadn't been visited since ancient times. No flowers grew here, nothing but tall weeds and mushrooms, pale, brown, spotty, thin, fat and short and bulbous. Hermana's grandmother had taught them how to tell the poisonous ones from the good ones, but she didn't know what they were called in books. Even Hermana, with her two whole years of schooling, couldn't name

4

more than three of them. So they'd named the rest themselves, Hermana coming up with the more imaginative—Devil's Candy, Star Dust, Spotted Templeroofs—and Ruth coming up with the more blandly descriptive names—Pretty Whites, Long Stalks, Fat Roundheads.

They found the corpse amidst a clump of Pretty Whites.

It was Ruth who discovered the body, stepping forward with her nose held high, sniffing vigorously, before jumping back with a high-pitched squeak. Apart from a number of bird calls she could pull off, Ruth was not known for high-pitched noises. Hermana looked up from the patch of Fat Roundheads she had been inspecting and then strode over to join her friend, who was standing stock-still with her elbows locked at her sides.

When Hermana saw what she was staring at, she half fell backwards, grabbing at Ruth's bony shoulder. "That's..."

"Shut up," Ruth hissed. Slowly, she took a tentative step forward, and then another.

From a distance, it could have been mistaken for another clump of Pretty Whites, sunken low enough into the soft ground that the tip of its nose rose no higher than the nearest mushroom. It lay on its back, one arm flung behind its head, the other across its abdomen. It might have been sleeping but for the fact its eyes were half-open and rolled back so they could only see the whites.

At that moment, Hermana worked out what had been bothering her since they first came into the glade. The birds weren't singing. Now that she listened, she realised she couldn't hear any mosquitoes either, nor any of the hundreds of buzzing, slithering, burrowing beasts that lived off the fungus patch.

"Bugger me. We've found a dead person, Ruth."

Ruth crouched down, her sharp knees digging into the mud, and touched it. Contrasted against the warm brown of Ruth's two fingers pressed against its neck, the corpse looked even paler. In fact, looking closely, Hermana thought that his skin had a greenish tinge to it. Was that normal?

Beyond its colouration, it had other odd features. It was more slender and delicate than any man Hermana had ever met—who,

5

admittedly, consisted of big brawny farmers and rugged merchants. Its hair was far longer than was respectable for a man, and its face (*his*, she thought, *he was a person, give him that much*) was bereft of pockmarks, acne scars, freckles, mosquito bites, and wrinkles. To Hermana, it looked more like a stone carving than a real face. As to his age, the best she could do was 'more than fifteen, less than fifty'.

"It's not wearing much, is it?" Ruth noted, and indeed, it was not. No shirt, no coat, no shoes, just a strip of pale cloth wrapped round its hips. Indecent, really. "Hey, look at those!"

She'd taken up a twig and used it to push back the dew-damp locks on either side of its face, enough to reveal the small gold rings dangling from the lobes of its ears. Both girls drew in breath, and Hermana gave a low whistle. Neither of their families owned jewellery. The only earrings they had ever seen belonged to the fancy folk who passed through the forest on horseback to get to their mountain retreats.

"Now where did it get those?" Ruth murmured, her eyes bright with a magpie-gleam. "If it was robbed, they'd have been taken."

"Maybe it...*he* wasn't robbed," said Hermana. She swallowed, feeling it bounce in her throat. "Maybe he lost his clothes somewhere and froze."

"Don't be stupid. How would he lose his clothes? Maybe if he was swimming in the river and a badger made off with them, but then why would he come all the way up here?"

"To try to find the badger?"

"All right, so why was he swimming in the river in the middle of the night?"

"He must have frozen to death, though. Look. There's no marks on him."

It was true; his torso was as bare and unblemished as the rest of him. Hermana thought that the death wound might be on his back but didn't say so. She was too afraid Ruth might want to roll him over and have a look.

"No marks," Ruth said, tapping her chin. "Funny sort of colour. And he's ice cold, but he's not really stiff when you touch him. Go on. Touch him. You'll see what I mean."

6

"I'll take your word for it," Hermana grunted. "You think he died last night, then?"

Ruth trailed her thumb over the corpse's jawline. "Could be. Could be. The smell's a bit strong, don't you think? A smell like that, I'd have expected him to be at least a full day past his best."

Hermana's stomach roiled. Even though she was used to Ruth poking and prodding at odd things, she felt in her heart that you weren't supposed to prod a dead person. "Do you think he's a nobleman? Look at his arms; there's no muscle there at all. He's thin as a wisp. And those hands ain't got a single callous, do they? Only fancy folk can afford to look as prissy as that."

"None of our fancy folk dress like that, though," Ruth said doubtfully. "None of them have got long hair, either. 'S not fashionable. And if he's quality, where's his horse? I can count the number of times I've seen that lot dismount on one hand. You'd think their arses were nailed down."

"Maybe he's foreign. From the east. Gran says they eat their horses." Hermana wrapped her arms around her chest. "Shouldn't we tell someone, Ruthie?"

"Like who? Your gran? Don't see what good it would do, apart from rattling her nerves. She's got enough to worry about, what with that lout Gregor skulking around the house again."

"I meant the sheriff."

"Hah! To hell with that; she'll think we did it."

Raking her fingernails back through her short, curly hair—she'd been worrying for a few days that she'd picked up lice—Hermana nodded. "Then maybe we should tell...y'know. Them."

Hermana gestured upwards, in the direction of the pass beyond the crags.

"No. *Fuck* no."

Fifteen years ago, a wealthy merchant had lost his way in these woods and found himself up by the waterfalls on the other side of the mountain. The first question he had asked upon being found and rescued was how much the land was going for. When it had come to light that the mountain had no legal owner, he had dug a heel into his horse's

7

side and shot for the capital city, stopping for neither food nor rest.

Soon, there were sixteen chalets built up around the falls, and every year when the lavender started to blossom, a party of horsemen and carriages would traipse up the narrow road past Ruth and Hermana's homes, usually escorted by several big tough types with blunderbusses and swords across their backs. Down in the village, they celebrated the coming of spring with a feast and a bonfire. Up in the woods, Ruth and Hermana celebrated by hiding in the thick brush above the road and chucking acorns at the heads of the fancy folk.

"Worst-case scenario, it *is* one of that lot, and they drag us away for a beating when we tell 'em," said Ruth. "Best case, it's a foreigner, and they still drag us away for a beating because they think we've been selling him information."

Hermana scratched one of her ears. "What sort of information have we got to sell to foreigners?"

"Lots. Like, um, like how many pear trees the mayor planted this year."

"Foreigners would care about that, would they?"

"Of course they would, stupid. If you're planning on marching an army through these parts to lay siege to the capital, you need to know how many pear trees you're going to have to uproot on the way."

"Good point."

They lapsed into reflective silence.

"He's sort of good-looking, isn't he?" said Hermana, thoughtfully. "Not like the village boys, I mean. Like...like a crane, or a pricey horse."

"There's not one hair on his chin, even though he's well past his spotty years," observed Ruth. "Maybe he's a eunuch."

"What's that?"

"A bloke what's had his bits off. If he's done a rape and got caught, for example, or if he's in a church."

"If he's in a church? Why?"

Ruth shrugged. "You've got to have your bits off if you're in a church. It's the rule. I read it somewhere."

"Liar. You can't read."

They continued contemplating the corpse, which Hermana found,

8

she was now thinking of as *their* corpse. It was, above all else, interesting, and she and Ruth had long ago laid claim to all of the forest's most interesting properties. The view from the crags was their view. The stinging nettles into which Hermana had once fallen were their stinging nettles. The only bit that wasn't theirs was the road; that belonged to the village (which didn't preclude their terrorising anyone who dared set foot on it when they were bored).

Eventually, Ruth leaned over it again and pulled off both of its earrings with a sharp tug.

"Nice," she said, holding one up into a weak beam of sunlight. "This one's for you."

"What am I supposed to do with it?" Hermana asked, as the tiny gold thing was dropped into her palm.

"Put it in your ear, stupid. Or your nose, that'd be even better. You'd look like a pirate."

Hermana put the earring into her pocket. She didn't think she was tall enough to be a pirate. "We can flog these, can't we?"

"So long as no one asks where they came from."

"Fair point."

It was getting late. They'd arrived at the patch later than they normally did—Hermana had been nailing down a hole in Gran's roof all morning—and the thin slice of sky visible above the clearing was turning lavender. Night bugs would be out soon, and nastier things would follow. They scooped up handful of mushrooms, checking that they weren't poisonous and brushing off ants.

"We're agreed, then?" said Ruth. "We keep it to ourselves, right? We don't tell anyone. Not even Ned."

Hermana nodded. She loved Ruth's brother, but the thought of him coming into the grove, clambering over the Cod with his big boots and stomping about in the mushroom patch, was intolerable. This part of the woods was *theirs*.

"I s'pose it doesn't matter much," she said. "He'll rot fast enough. There's rain on the way. And the wolves'll have him in the night."

As they climbed over the Cod with a pocketful of mushrooms each, Ruth said, "Let's come back tomorrow and bury him. Ned said he'd bring some fancy apples back from the village today for us. We could eat them tomorrow to reward ourselves for getting him in the ground."

Hermana grinned. Most of her adventures into the world of exotic cuisine—cinnamon pastries and chocolate and fancy apples—had come courtesy of Ned's ability to haggle with merchants for treats. "Sounds fun. I'll wake up early to get my chores done."

The first of the fireflies were out by the time they were halfway down the slope. They'd taken the long way to the mushroom patch, the path that lead past the river in which Hermana had drowned when she was twelve. Ruth, five months younger but stronger and taller already, had pulled her out and pounded on her chest until she'd vomited up a lungful of water and duckweed. Three of her ribs had cracked beneath Ruth's small fists. Within a month, she'd been following her strange new friend up the mountain for the first time.

Hermana tensed as the smell of expensive leather and horse reached her nostrils.

"Hello, doves. Should you two be walking alone?"

"Nothing scarier around here than us," said Ruth, a lazy, insolent smile sliding over her face. "Hello, Daniel."

The boy beaming down at them from atop a gorgeous black stallion had a neat beard, cut to accentuate his pronounced cheekbones, and he wore a rakish, wide-brimmed hat. At his side, Hermana spotted the handle of a dagger, in a rakishly expensive silver scabbard, and she scowled as he gave Ruth a rakish wink.

Unlike most of the rich snots who came racing up the mountain each spring, Daniel had a modicum of sense in his head. Most of his friends from the capital—he seemed to bring a new pack with him every year—wore gold chains, restrictive and tight pants with no pockets on them, and soft, billowing shirts which showed off their upper arms. Not Daniel; his jackets were always new and spotless, but at least they looked like they might stand up to a sudden downpour or a swarm of hornets. His father had sent him to the front lines for a year when he had turned eighteen, and the hands that gripped the reins were properly calloused, the face that beamed down on them suntanned. One thing he did have in common with other fancy boys was his taste in hats, all of which were

10

huge and feathered. Today's hat made him look like a dashing pirate captain.

In a smooth, practised gesture, he plucked it off and drew it to his breast, performing an elegant half bow in the saddle, without once breaking eye contact with Ruth. All told, the amount of attention he had dedicated to Hermana in all the years they'd known him was slightly less than equal to the sum of the attention he lavished upon Ruth's knees every time he looked at her. Hermana returned the favour and kept her attention on his horse. It was larger than any horse she had ever seen before, which made it larger than any animal she had seen before, barring that bear.

"Ruth, Ruth," Daniel murmured, running his eyes appreciatively over her bare stomach. "How I've missed you. You know, every time I see you, you get taller and taller."

"Every time I see you, your horse gets taller and taller," Ruth rejoined. "This is your fifth one, you spoiled louse. How many d'you have?"

"This? This isn't mine, this is Father's," he said, patting the animal's mane. "They were training him up to be a warhorse. He's gutless, though. Can't stand loud noises. Still, he's a sight, isn't he?"

Hermana didn't hate many things. She hated wildfires, which had been a recurring nightmare since she was ten. The village boy who had spat at her that one time—she hated him. The dog his father had set on her after she'd punched his face—him, too. Most everything else, she either liked or didn't care about.

She *hated* Daniel, had hated him ever since he'd charged in on his great big stupid horse three years ago and frightened off the bear that had been chasing them. Ever since Ruth had started giving him her insolent, indulgent smiles. His family had a chalet near the falls, with a great wall wrapped around it and an iron gate wider than Hermana's house. His full name was eight syllables long, and his father was an earl. He was, by his own account, thirty-first in line for the throne (or thirty-second; Hermana had a habit of finding other things to pay attention to when Daniel began talking).

None of which Hermana would have minded all that much if it

hadn't been for the way he looked at Ruth. The way he was currently looking at Ruth.

Ruth, for her part, was preoccupied with the horse. "He's a beauty. What's his name? And how old is he? And what's the fastest he can run?"

Mute and scowling, Hermana endured five minutes of horse talk, waiting for the inevitable.

"I'm headed up to the old shack," Daniel said casually. Hermana had seen the old shack once or twice (from the outside, of course). It was three stories high and had its own chapel. "Father's expecting me. Now that I'm of age, everything's much more complicated. I do envy you girls sometimes, you know. It must be nice to have nothing expected of you. Still, it's not all bad, being home. The garden will be in full bloom, and Father's peach trees are splendid this time of year. I don't think I've ever shown you the peach trees, have I, Ruth?"

"No, don't think you have," said Ruth.

"Ah. Well, you should come along some time. With me, I mean. It's a treat, it really is. I complain, but I do love the old place. And my aunts would be mad about you; they're starved for company, and they approve of healthy girls. I could take you there any time you liked. Perhaps I could even show you the stables. We've got a foal on the way."

Unbidden, Ruth's mouth broke apart into a wide grin, the sort she usually reserved for Hermana's better jokes. "No lying? A foal?"

Damn him, Hermana thought. *Damn him and his hat all the way to hell.*

When girls in the village turned fifteen, the village boys would make them flower crowns. The prettiest got the best crowns, made of hollyhocks and lilies and primroses, if they hadn't bled yet. The ugly, the abrasive, and the odd would receive crowns of daisies or dandelions, if they were lucky, from their fathers or some other well-meaning male relative. It was one of those ridiculously twee traditions that the tourists liked, but it wasn't all for show. Getting a lot of crowns meant that your prospects were good, that you'd have your pick of several husbands and your parents could breathe easy. Getting a dandelion crown let everyone know that you'd have to take what you were given, and that might mean marrying poorer, might mean that your bride price wouldn't cover the cost of the proper ceremony, might mean that your husband wouldn't feel obliged to take care of your mother and father. A lot of the girls who received dandelion crowns ending up leaving the village for the coastal towns or the capital, where there were more opportunities for unwed women.

Hermana knew, and had known since she was small, that there would be no flower crown for her. All the village blokes knew her at a glance as the bastard granddaughter of the old woman who lived up the mountain, and subsequent years of stealing their apples and chucking acorns at their heads had done nothing to shift their opinion. They were all useless, anyway, either too snotty or too boring to bother with. She had no father, nor any living male relatives to go matchmaking for her, and Gran had never shown any inclination to broach the topic. She had just sort of assumed that she would live on the mountain forever with Ruth; when Gran got too frail to make her regular trips down to the village to offer her services, she would teach Hermana how to midwife and prepare her special ointments and potions. And life would proceed as it always had.

Ruth had never received a flower crown, either—Ned was no good at making them—and it wasn't until Daniel had entered the picture that it had occurred to Hermana that she might not be happy with this state of affairs.

Daniel nodded. "As I say, you should come visit. I'll be down this way again in a day or so—need to get some fishing in, I'm out of practice—and you can come back home with me then, if you like. Up to you."

He glanced at the sky and then said, "I say... Are you busy now, Ruth?"

"Yes," said Hermana.

"No," said Ruth, poking her in the ribs.

"Well, as it happens, neither am I. I've got an hour before I'm due to meet Father for dinner. Would you like a ride?"

She gaped. "On...on him? Right now?"

"Of course!" Daniel beamed. "I can't promise he won't stumble— he's not familiar with your woods yet—but you're a tough girl, aren't

13

you? Keep your arms around my waist, and you'll be fine. I'm an experienced horseman."

"Brilliant! Hermie, you come behind me."

Daniel blinked while Ruth climbed into the saddle behind him. Hermana wasn't tall enough and needed to clutch Daniel's arm as she came up. To her disgust, she found that it was firm and sinewy, putting paid to her hopes that he really was a useless fancy boy and all his riding and fishing were for show.

"Thank you," she said stiffly, as Ruth laughed and held tight to Daniel's shoulders.

"It's so high!" she exulted. "Danny, make him gallop!"

As they left the path and set out through the conifers, Hermana was forced to admit that riding a cantering warhorse was pretty brilliant. Daniel led them up to the crags where the wind whistled night and day, and Hermana hollered with excitement as they ran along the edge of the cliff. Looking down, she could see the whole valley spread out beneath them.

Such was the valley's shape that local legend held it to have been created by the stomp of a club-footed giant. It was, Hermana had always thought, much better looking from up here. The lake was grand enough to make the village an afterthought, a murky brown smudge beside a wide, white mirror. The fields of barley and wheat looked artful and lovely from above, a perfect contrast to the densely forested wilderness that overran the rest of the valley. Across the winding expanse of the river, a shepherd the size of a flea directed sheep the size of sand grains toward a bridge. The main road lay like a tan snake, disappearing into the tree line by Donkey Pass, the only way out of the valley. Hermana's grandmother had said that it would lead you straight to the capital if you followed it for long enough, and straight to the sea after that.

When they came to a halt, Hermana rubbed the horse's side in thanks, and she dismounted flushed and exuberant. Ruth took a moment to disengage the death grip she had on Daniel's jacket and came down on wobbly legs, distinctly green at the gills.

"Thank you for the pleasure of your company, doves," he said, tipping his hat. He waved at them as he departed and rode out of view, his short cape billowing behind him.

"You all right?" Hermana said. "You go any more pale, and you're going to turn into a spook."

"If you look at Daniel any more sour, you're going to turn into a lemon," Ruth countered, leaning against her for support. "How difficult do you think it is to nick a foal?"

"Think the difficult part's finding somewhere to keep it."

It was twilight by the time they reached the road that cut the forest in half. In fair weather, it would take either of them five minutes to walk from Hermana's secluded house to Ruth's, which sat higher up the road. By the time the light of Hermana's grandmother's fireplace became visible, so too was the shape of the roof Ruth's brother had spent last summer repairing, silhouetted against the purple sky.

"Gran said she was cooking rabbit. You hungry?" Hermana asked.

"Bloody hell, I *really* am."

Chapter Two

Even in summer, it got wickedly cold on the mountainside at night, although snow was a rare occurrence. Her grandmother's house was a little fortress of warmth and light.

As they approached it, Ruth slowed, squinted, and then spat.

"Balls," muttered Hermana. "Not again."

Four men stood in Gran's vegetable patch, one holding open a brown sack while the other three ripped up handfuls of radishes and cabbage. A fifth stood by the front door, his hands clasped at his front, as though he was expecting to be invited in. Hermana regarded his stance and the set of his shoulders, and came to the conclusion that he was pissing on the doorstep.

"Gregor," said Ruth.

He turned as he heard them approach, a droplet of urine still clinging to his big pink prick. Sneering as his gaze crossed from Ruth's angry face to her mud-smeared knees, he whistled, and the other four looked over.

"Hello, little Ruby," he said. Hermana had never worked out if he didn't know their names, or if he couldn't be bothered using them.

As Ruth's fists balled, Hermana inspected the villagers. Not drunk, she didn't think, just bored. They were all strong, broad men—farmhands—and they all had the same blotchy skin, trimmed moustaches, and messy neck stubble common to the men of Mar Reilly. The stink of urine wafted over to her, and she wrinkled her nose. Gregor came forward, his prick still loose, waving from side to side like a baby bird at feeding time.

"You're a sight, my girl," he said to Ruth, taking on a fatherly tone of disapproval. "Playing about in the mud all day like you're ten, come back home looking like you've been humped by a bear. Where's the big

17

bastard of a brother of yours? Didn't he teach you better?"

Like he was approaching a riled skunk, Gregor crept closer by increments. The other four abandoned the vegetable patch and spread out, folding large, meaty arms over large, barrel chests. If she and Ruth turned on their heels right now, Hermana thought, they could lose them in the trees. Village folk couldn't navigate the woods for shit, and even though Hermana was a slower runner than Ruth, she was still faster than most people.

Ruth didn't budge an inch, not even when he came to loom over her.

"Don't frown like that, Ruby-girl. You'll ruin your pretty face. Give us a smile, eh?"

He bent down, his strong jaw and sun-browned nose in her face. He wouldn't rape them, Hermana thought. He knew better. He might well rough them up, though, or... Yes, there went his hand, running down the edge of Ruth's breast like he was petting a dog. Stone-faced, Ruth still didn't move.

Cursing them both, Hermana opened her mouth to scream. They'd punch her for it before they ran, but at least it would get things over with quicker. She was hungry.

Before she could make a sound, Gregor choked and froze in place. The edge of a well-honed kitchen knife pressed against his throat.

"Nothing I hate more than bad manners," said a quiet voice from behind him.

There were people in the village who believed that Hermana's grandmother was a witch. Most of the time, it wasn't a problem; Maggie Dim was the best midwife for miles around, and whenever she went down to visit her clients, she did a brisk trade in cunningly devised ointments for burns, cuts, and mosquito bites. Her skill and her reputation had earned her a lot of leeway from the village priest and his cronies.

Contemptuous as she was of proper folk and their dull-witted superstitions, Hermana had to admit that if she hadn't been related to Maggie Dim, she might well have thought the same. Her grandmother's nose was long and hooked. Her eyebrows flared at the edges, giving the impression of a barn owl in a scrubby apron. She was tall for a woman, her steel-grey bun brushing the top of the door frame when she strode

18

outside each morning to feed the chickens. Her age was difficult to determine—every birthday, Hermana would try a new, unsuccessful trick to weasel it out of her—for the deep lines beneath her eyes were belied by the lack of liver spots on her hands and the strength of her grip.

She had a clump of Gregor's hair clenched in her fist. The other four men exchanged looks, uncertain of what to do. They knew that, regardless of what else was said about her, Maggie Dim had never murdered anyone. Likely as not, she wasn't about to open Gregor's throat in front of them. On the other hand, no one wanted to be the first to go over and use their big, meaty arms to get her off him. This was Maggie Dim. Pissing on her doorstep was one thing; *touching* her was another.

"Ruth, Hermana, come here," she barked, and they scurried to her side. "Mister Markbridge, I want you to leave, and I want your friends to leave. And I don't want to see you again. Take the veggies, if you must. But the next time you lay hands on my girl or her friend" —her grip tightened; Gregor's eyes watered— "I'll be having a word with your mother. Fixed up her back last month. S'pect she's grateful."

"Me mum's a drunken tart," snarled Gregor, rallying. "And you're a fucking hag."

"Hermana, kick his shin," said Maggie, and Hermana did so.

As Gregor yelped and clutched his leg, she pushed him away. "Off you go, Mister Markbridge. Best hurry up. It's a long way down, and nobody likes being up the mountain after dark."

He didn't say a word more; just grunted at his friends and turned to limp down the road. In dribs and drabs, they followed after him, casting black looks back at Maggie and the girls. Hermana waited until they were dots before letting out her breath.

Ruth spat. "Scum."

Maggie sighed and wiped her brow. "Thought we were in for it, for a moment there."

She tilted her nose and sniffed. "Dear me. I think Mister Markbridge might have an infection brewing in his pipes. Don't fancy smelling that all through dinner. Ruthie, your boy hungry?"

19

Ruth's brother Ned was chopping wood when they arrived at her house.

Ned was handsome enough, broad shouldered and long legged, with a soft, unhappy smile. Though his skin was too dark for him to make a wife of a farmer's daughter, he'd have been a catch for any of the pretty servant girls who worked in the big houses down below. Once, long ago, Ruth had suggested that Hermana marry him when she turned seventeen, as 'Then we'd be like real sisters'. She'd lived in fear of the prospect for ages, until Ned had sat her down and explained to her that he had absolutely no interest in marrying her or any other girl, and that this was one of the main reasons they only welcomed him down in the village when there was work to be done.

"Hello, Maggie," he said with a nod. "Is that a rabbit I spy?"

"It is indeed, love," she said, kissing his cheek. "Ruth, Hermana, you go wash your hands while I get this in the pot."

Ruth's parents had abandoned both their children before she could walk, and for most of Ruth's childhood, the house had been ruled by her uncle. When his heart had failed him two weeks after her tenth birthday, she and Ned had buried him several feet deeper than was necessary. They'd burned the sheets on which he'd died and poured his liquor out onto the dirt. Lastly, they'd found his belt, and even though it was still good, strong leather and they could have traded it for food, they'd cut it up into a dozen pieces and thrown them in the river.

The last thing of his they'd thrown away had been his surname. It had been Ruth who had decided on 'Honeyduck' as a replacement; Ned agreed to it because it made Ruth laugh. He was all right with anything that made Ruth laugh, which was why he was so accommodating of her many invertebrate pets and jars with things floating in them. Consequently, Hermana had carved the new family surname into the lintel above the front door in wide, uneven letters, for neither Ruth nor her brother could write.

The girls went to wash up in the tub of cold water behind the house, flicking away mosquitoes and night bugs. They had one thin sliver of soap that had to last the next two months at least, and they shared it judiciously.

20

"We've got to bury him," said Ruth.

Scrubbing behind her ears with a halfway bald brush, Hermana said, "Never buried a person before."

"It'll be easy as pie. People weigh less than you'd think. Uncle was a big fat bastard, and me and Ned didn't have any trouble with him. This one's such a scrawny bugger, I could probably lift him myself. The hardest part will be digging the hole. You've got to get it deep enough or sometimes they rise up. Can you nick your gran's shovel?"

"What? Oh... Yeah, yeah. Not a problem." Hermana was distracted by Ruth's bare back. It had three large moles, two on her left shoulder blade and one lower down, arranged in roughly the same shape as the dim constellation her grandmother called 'the Pitchfork'. Hermana told herself that that was what had drawn her attention, not the droplets of water running off Ruth's dark hair, down her neck, and towards the small of her back.

She was also conscious of her own flatter chest and shorter legs and tried to angle her body in such a way as to make them less apparent. *Stupid*, she told herself; they'd been swimming together starkers in the river since they were kids. They knew everything about one another's bodies, every wart and callous. And it wasn't as though Ruth was also sneaking peeks.

Not that she would, Hermana thought. Ruth wasn't a peeker. If Ruth wanted to look at something, she'd just look at it, as long and as hard as she wanted.

Drying herself, Hermana said, "Do you think we should...?"

"What?"

"Well, it's... We don't know what he'd... Is there something we should say, do you think? When we bury him? I mean, what if he *is* foreign, and there's some sort of funeral ritual we don't know about? I don't like the thought of some sod's ghost floating around the woods forever because we didn't do it right."

Ruth lapsed into silence, chewing her lip. Neither of them was remotely religious, but they both believed in ghosts. Slowly, she said, "I don't think there's that many ways you can do it, are there? It's pretty basic stuff, sticking a person in the ground. I know how they do it down

21

in the village, and I know how we did it when my uncle died. You stick 'em in, you pray, you wash your hands twice, and you're done. Not easy to muck that up."

Hermana's grandmother called them in to supper, and they devoured their stew in silence as the adults made conversation.

"Are your feet feeling any better, Maggie?" asked Ned.

"Not so bad as they were, love. Thank you," she sighed. "Very nasty few days, that was. I'll tell you this, Ned; don't ever think you can win a war against the flesh. No one can. All you can hope to do is outlast it. Hermana, love, you're awfully quiet. Is something wrong?"

"Nothing, Gran. I'm just thinking about dead people. Um. Not anyone specific. Dead people and...and death in general."

Ruth kicked her under the table.

"Ah," Maggie nodded sagely. "I did that a lot at your age. Used to brood over it for days. It'll pass. You'll find it becomes less important the older you get."

"By the way, your Daniel was round here this morning," Ned said to Ruth.

Ruth didn't look up from her stew. "That so? We met him in the woods a few hours ago. What was he doing here, then?"

"He wanted to talk to you. That's what he said. And he left that."

Ned pointed to the roses standing in a cracked pot on their windowsill, their petals a pale pink that put Hermana in mind of baby rats.

Ruth maintained a neutral expression. "What am I supposed to do with those?"

Ned shrugged. "It's a nice gesture; that's all. I liked him. Good clothes. Good teeth. I think you should hear him out, Ruth. It can't do any harm. He's not a bad man. I wouldn't want a bad man for you. You know that."

"Ned, you don't know a thing about him. And I *would* have heard him out, if there'd been anything to hear. He's not made it clear yet what he's after."

"You're not stupid, so don't pretend like it," Ned snapped and rubbed his forehead. "I'm not trying to be a bully, Ruth; I swear I'm not.

22

You can't deny it would make life a lot easier if one of us pulled off a respectable marriage."

"And it plainly ain't going to be you," she said flatly.

"Now, look..." he started, and Maggie banged her mug on the table.

"No fighting at dinner," she said. "Ruth, your brother only wants what's best for you. Ned, your sister's a better judge of character than you are. If she doesn't want him, that's an end of it. There's dozens of other rich boys prancing their ponies about on this mountain."

"At least promise me that you'll be polite, Ruthie?" Ned pleaded.

"Polite as pie," she promised. "I might see him again tomorrow. Me and Hermie are going back up the slope. We think we might have found a quail nest. Long time since we've had quail eggs, eh?"

"You two go up there so often, anyone would think you had secret fellows," muttered Maggie, and then she laughed at Ned's stricken expression. It said a lot about Ruth's brother that this possibility had not occurred to him before.

"I ain't got a fellow," Ruth said, rolling her eyes.

Well, not one's who's liable to knock either of us up, at any rate, thought Hermana, smiling into her bowl.

Later, as the Dims were about to leave, Ruth hissed in Hermana's ear, "Tomorrow, all right? We'll get it done right quick. It'll be a doddle. Don't you worry."

Chapter Three

The following morning, Hermana came awake with a violent start an hour before dawn. Fragments of a nightmare in which Ruth's naked body had taken the place of the strange green man—lying in the mushroom patch amidst roses the colour of baby rats—were scattered about the inside of her head. She got up and walked around the house until they'd gone.

The home she shared with her grandmother offered far more space than either of them needed. Maggie had told her that it had once been a tavern, or the makings of a tavern, before its intended owner had died and left the work unfinished. Stupid place for one, anyway; all the merchants and messengers who came this way stayed in the inn down in the village. Besides being too big for them, the house was dilapidated, scarcely fit for human habitation at the best of times. The floorboards were too rotted to stand on in a dozen places, and there were so many draughts in winter that being inside was as bad as being out. They kept it clean, at least; the two of them were naturally inclined to tidiness.

Hermana busied herself sweeping the floor and shooing out a beetle, and then she crept through to Maggie's bed and plucked the small, sleeping hog from its customary position on her feet. Her grandmother bestowed the sort of affection on the animal that Hermana supposed ordinary women did on their firstborn sons. Today, it accompanied Hermana to the stream as the first line of gold fell across the mountain's peak, trotting at her side as faithfully as any hound. She wrung out three pairs of socks and filled a bucket for Maggie to clean her face and feet in. On the way back to the house, she spotted a poorly constructed nest in the branches of a chestnut and shimmied up to retrieve it.

By the time her grandmother staggered out of bed, the smell of scrambled eggs and mushrooms wafted through the house.

"I told Ruth I'd meet her in a little while," Hermana said, as she presented Maggie with her breakfast. "Anything you need done first?"

"I think we've got a bat in the attic; could you see if you can get it out?" said Maggie.

The bat turned out to be a raccoon, and catching it was the work of forty minutes and a heavy stick.

"Lovely," said Maggie, taking it from her. "I've been needing a new pair of slippers. Dress up warmly, dear. It might rain today."

Before leaving, Hermana procured her grandmother's heavy bastard of a shovel and, as an afterthought, a pair of thick leather gloves.

❋❋❋

Ruth was up against the hickory when Hermana found her, scratching her signature into its grey bark with a rock. Because Ruth had never learned letters, her signature consisted of a wobble-edged oblong, with six lines protruding from its centre, and two short lines protruding from a smaller circle attached to its tip. There were several hundred trees throughout the forest bearing Ruth's mark, and Hermana suspected that it was her friend's intention to have marked every one of them by the time she died.

A shovel stood propped against the trunk. As Hermana approached, Ruth looked up, and Hermana started. "Bloody hell, Ruth, what've you done?"

The taller girl grinned and tilted her head from side to side. Sunlight flashed off the gold in her right ear. "Not bad, is it?"

"What'd Ned say? How'd you do it?" She leaned in to take a closer look. The hole in Ruth's earlobe was neatly made, and the earring had been cleaned and polished. It did, in fact, make her look like a pirate.

"That's why my hair's loose; so he won't notice. If he does, I'm going to say I found it on the road. He'll think one of the quality dropped it. I used a sewing needle, it was dead easy. I can do you too, if you like."

"Later," Hermana said hurriedly. "Let's go."

"Righto. I've already picked out a spot."

The forest was unusually quiet today. No bird song, no insects

26

skittering underfoot. They didn't race up, but moved with quick, steady steps.

The spot Ruth had chosen for the grave was just outside the mushroom patch.

"I figure we want him out of the way, but I don't fancy carrying him far. And no one ever comes here but us," Ruth said.

After half an hour's digging, Hermana was panting like a dog and sweating like a hog. Their progress was slowed by the way Ruth kept stopping to pluck out little creatures they'd unearthed and inspect them. Finally, when the hole was deep enough for both of them to stand up in, they stopped.

When they walked up to the mushroom patch, the smell was stronger than it had been yesterday, and Ruth buried her nose in her shirt. Brushing the leaves away, they found that their new friend hadn't accumulated any maggots overnight.

"Hello, Mister Stiffy," said Ruth, taking out the apples stuffed in her pocket and giving one to Hermana before biting into her own. Swallowing, she commented, "No way Ned could afford these. He nicked 'em. Or whored for 'em. He says there's a lot of old dears down there who like to play with his hair."

Hermana made a face. "That's sort of *ick*, isn't it?"

Ruth shrugged. "His hair. He can do what he likes with it."

As they ate, they crossed slowly from one end of the glade to the other, trying once again to spot any clues that might identify their corpse.

"No weapons, no clothes left lying about, no hoof prints," Ruth reported. "No footprints from him, either. Weird."

"Maybe he's an assassin," said Hermana, who had once read a book in which just such an individual had been hired to murder a young king. She remembered being significantly more invested in the dashing rogue with a black silk cape than in any of the protagonists, and hoping that he would carry out his mission successfully, win his reward, and run off with the bereft queen. "They can walk in a special way, so's they don't leave footprints. And they can go invisible."

"You'd think an assassin would wear gloves, though. Or at least pants. And he's not carrying a weapon. What sort of person goes wandering about the wilderness without pants or weapons?"

"Maybe he ate one of the mushrooms. The bad ones, I mean," said Hermana, crouching down beside their friend. "That would have finished him off."

"Could be. I'd have expected to find dried vomit or blood or something. And it still doesn't explain what he was doing here in the first place."

"Maybe he assassinated someone, and then he came here to hide away until the coast was clear."

"If... Wait a minute. What's that?"

Ruth pointed to the corpse's ankle. No—following her gaze, Hermana saw that she was pointing to the patch of earth surrounding the ankle. Instead of the dark, loamy hue that characterised the soil in this part of the woods, it had gone a pale yellow, reminiscent of cat vomit.

Frowning, Hermana reached forward and took up a pinch of it. "It's... Ugh. What *is* it?"

Pressing it between forefinger and thumb, she found that it had a strange, tar-like texture, not unlike the cold porridge that her grandmother specialised in on those days when it was her turn at breakfast: slimy and compromised of irregular-sized lumps and suspicious flecks of grit suggestive of a badly cleaned pot. She tried rolling it into a ball and then stretching it. It didn't seem to absorb any of the warmth from her palm. After a minute of investigative prodding, it was still as cold as a fish snatched straight from the river. When she clenched her hand, it didn't crumble between her fingers so much as *squish,* dropping down to the ground with a soft, wet 'splat'.

"That's what the smell's coming from," Ruth said and leaned back over the corpse. She sniffed the bare skin of its knee and then sniffed the yellowish dirt around its ankles. "Yeah, that's it. That stink's coming from the yellow stuff, not off the body."

They found another clump of it beneath the corpse's right knee, where they also found a dead beetle. Its wings were spread, as though it had been trying to take off, and its body was covered in pale yellow flecks. When Hermana picked it up, she found that the stuff had hardened upon the carapace and trying to pick it off only chipped her fingernails. Continuing their investigation, they found more, three patches by its shoulders, and one beneath either elbow.

"What the hell is it, Ruth?" Hermana said, poking a dead caterpillar that had attempted to crawl over the largest patch.

"Hell if I know," said Ruth. She had returned her attention to the corpse's face and was busy pushing back its pale green upper lip.

"Ruth, mate, I don't think you should go poking and prodding at a person you don't know," said Hermana uneasily.

"I don't think it's a person."

"It *was* a person," Hermana amended.

"No, I mean... Look at its teeth."

Hermana had, in fact, noticed its teeth and had been trying very hard to pretend she hadn't.

"Not a single one missing or rotten," said Ruth. "And they're white as snow, all of them. Not even fancy folk have teeth like that."

"You're going to make me say it, ain't you?" Hermana said glumly. "They're sharp like razors, Ruthie. He's got fox teeth."

"Well, yeah. There's that. There's also this."

Delicately, Ruth drew back a lock of its hair, first exposing the pierced earlobe, then the concha, and then the hitherto concealed tip. The *pointy* tip.

Chapter Four

On the upside, Hermana reflected, this freed her from any lingering sense of responsibility to tell the authorities about their new friend.

"If *anyone* finds out about this, we're in it up to our necks," she said. "You know how the villagers are about...about this sort of business. Their priest never stops banging on about the evils of the occult and what have you. They find out we've got a genuine elf or pixie or whatever the sod is on our hands, who knows what they'll do? They might burn the whole forest down."

Ruth nodded. "One more reason to stick him in the ground before anyone pokes their noses in. You take his feet, I'll take his shoulders. Okay, here we go. Bend your knees. One, two, three! Oh, *bugger*."

"What the hell?" mumbled Hermana, staring at the corpse's feet. She wrapped her gloved hands around either ankle and tried again to lift it. Then she put both hands on one ankle and tried a third time.

"Is he stuck on something?" Ruth said, after several similarly fruitless attempts to shift the corpse's head. "I can't budge him an inch. It's like he's been nailed down."

They checked and ascertained that there was nothing for him to be stuck on.

"Is it the yellow muck that's sticking him to the ground, do you think?" Hermana wondered.

"Can't be. I'm standing in it, and I've no problem lifting my feet. I think he's just heavy."

"How can anyone be *that* heavy? He's so thin!"

They tried again, and again, and again. Finally, panting, they gave up.

"Let's...let's just see if we can roll him," said Ruth.

They couldn't. Together, straining and cursing, they both tried to

31

lift one of his slender, elegant hands.

After five minutes, Ruth collapsed back onto the ground and groaned. "Damn it, Hermie. What're we going to do?"

Hermana picked a piece of apple skin from her teeth. "It's a puzzler, isn't it? Here, I've had a thought. We might've been a bit stupid. What if it wasn't the mushrooms that finished him off? What if he was sick? What if he makes *us* sick?"

Abruptly, Ruth stood. "Well reasoned, Dim. Let's go wash our hands before we try anything else."

As soon as they were out of the mushroom patch, Hermana sucked in a lungful of clean air. She hadn't realised how awful the stink had become.

On the way down to the river, she noticed that jingle of fast-flowing water that typically echoed through the woods had subsided to a tired murmur. She arrived at the water's edge first and threw out an arm to stop Ruth from coming any closer. They stood in silence for some time.

A yellowish film had collected on the surface of the water, whose motion had slowed to a crawl, as though it were honey or thickening blood. A heron staggered on the opposite bank, either too disoriented to know they were there or too sickly to take flight. A single dead fish lay half-in, half-out of the water, its scales dulled and covered with yellow flecks, and as they watched, three more floated past.

"Fuck," Hermana breathed. "When did...?"

Ruth squinted up at the canopy, dappled light falling across her face. "We're going to need a new plan, Hermie."

Chapter Five

Katie Bellows eyed the overhanging bowers and thrust out a long stick before her. She walked like a blind woman, poking and prodding the overgrown path with every cautious step.

"They're more afraid of you than you are of them... They're more afraid of you than you are of them," she chanted under her breath. She wasn't sure whether she was talking about the snakes and other horrid beasties that inhabited these woods, or the people she was on her way to visit.

To the devil with the outdoors, she thought moodily, cursing the fresh air, the bugs, and the mud coating the undersides of her boots. How unpleasant it all was. How *untidy* everything was. Katie was not, by nature, sure-footed, even on cobblestones or the perfectly flat lawn that dominated Mistress's prize-winning garden, never mind walking uphill, encumbered with two heavy baskets. Every time she was forced to go trotting up the mountain slope, she tripped on a root or a rock and got grass stains on her dress. When that happened, one of two choices opened up before her: return to the manor on time with a stained dress, and receive six lashes and half portions at dinner, or return late after spending an hour washing out the stain and drying the dress, and receive four lashes, and no dinner.

The faster we get there, the sooner we go home, she told herself, for the baskets were making her arms ache, and she was sorely tempted to put them down for a moment.

A shadow fell across the path, and she looked up. On the verge above her, two figures had appeared, silhouetted against the single beam of sunlight that penetrated the branches overhead. Both were wearing wide fox grins.

"Look who it is," said the taller one. "A little lost sheep. What's it

33

doing here, all alone?"

The shorter one, who always looked hunch-shouldered and sly, had her hand behind her back, hiding something. Katie was one of those people for whom dread often translated into gastrointestinal distress, and now her stomach roiled.

They were about five years younger than she was, and Katie was stronger than she looked—you had to be, to weather Mistress's moods for as long as she had. But she wasn't a match for both of them, and she couldn't outrun them, not here. She took a deep breathe to compose herself, and put the baskets down in front of her.

"Charity for you," she said.

Of course it wasn't her place to say so, but she didn't agree with Mistress's decision to direct her humanitarian efforts away from the village's Carthorse Protection Society and towards the filthy, half-civilised residents of the forest. Inside the baskets were four sets of baby blankets, four sets of good Sunday shoes, little Jamie's waistcoat, little Agatha's best dress, little Maureen's toy elephant, little David's comb, and a huge array of childhood paraphernalia, all set aside by children who had now left the house and the village. If Mistress had asked her, Katie would have politely suggested that perhaps the thuggish mountain girls wouldn't have much use for waistcoats and toy elephants, and that perhaps Katie's own younger brother might appreciate such tokens more.

Mistress hadn't asked her. And Katie had not survived twenty years in the manor by offering unsolicited advice.

"With Mistress's blessing," she said and made to depart.

"We have a present for your mistress," announced the taller one.

"She doesn't need your presents. It's charity. Charity doesn't need to be repaid."

The short, sly one folded her arms. "If your mistress is giving us presents, she should accept our presents. 'S rude not too."

"Very rude," agreed the taller one.

Their eyes glinted. *Like vermin,* Katie thought. She shivered. "All right. Give me your present."

Better to get it over with.

34

"Here you go!" shouted the shorter one, and her hand came out from behind her back. What she flung landed bare inches from the edge of Katie's dress. Katie's nose registered the smell first, and then she gave a shriek and fell back.

It was a pelt, at least two day's old, stripped off a red fox and covered in flies and some foul yellow muck. Foxes smelt bad enough when they were alive; two days' worth of decay was enough to make Katie's head spin. Her mouth opened and shut, trying to find words and hold back vomit all at once.

"Lovely beastie," grinned the taller one, eyes bright like a demon. "Caught it ourselves, just for your mistress. You take it to her. Tell her we say thank you."

There were a lot of rules to being a servant in the one of the village's fancier houses. The most important ones weren't written down anywhere. Katie had had to work them out for herself. For example, one very important rule was that no matter how much she or any of the other maids didn't like it, if a member of the family got tipsy and put his hand up their dresses, they weren't allowed to say anything. Another important rule was that if dear silly old Mister Whiskers knocked the milk over and drank all of it, they had to pretend that one of them had done it. Perhaps the most important unwritten rule was that if someone who wasn't a servant told them to do something, they did it, unless Mistress had explicitly told them not to.

The mountain girls were coarse, feral, and uneducated. They were, in Katie's opinion, something close to pure evil. But they weren't servants. They were betters.

You didn't tell betters where they could stick their gifts.

Katie looked at the stinking pelt and squeezed her eyes shut tight. Bending down, she took hold of it by its tail, trying to pretend it was a dish cloth. Holding it at arm's length, she managed a small, formal nod to the girls. They weren't high-born, so it was, technically, sufficient. Besides, if she'd tried to thank them properly, with a curtsey, she would have thrown up.

With sweat starting to pour down her brow as the stench became inescapable, she turned and started off down the path, leaving the

35

baskets behind her.

"Bye, little sheep," sang the taller one, as the shorter one began to laugh. "See you later."

The walk back down took half an hour and felt as though it took all day. By the time she reached the garden gate, she was swaying from side to side. She gave the present to Freddie, the head gardener—just because you had to accept gifts from betters didn't mean you had to hand those gifts over to your mistress, particularly if you knew what Mistress's reaction would be to receiving a dirty bit of days-old vermin. He buried it too deep for Mistress's hounds to dig up, and then he gave her a cup of tea and a hug.

Chapter Six

There was a sock in her mouth and a stone digging into her back.

"Keep still," Ruth ordered, her brow furrowed in concentration.

From this vantage point, Hermana had an excellent view of Ruth's nostrils. She was uncomfortably aware of how much daintier they were than her own.

"It'll only hurt for a second; then it's done," said Ruth.

To avoid having to look at the red-hot needle she was holding, Hermana concentrated on her face. She'd never seen it this close before and was astonished to find that there were things about Ruth's countenance that she had not known. Her hair was tied back so that it didn't get in the way, revealing a scar right at the top of her forehead, no bigger than a bitten-off fingernail. How long had it been there? Since she was a child? Had her uncle been the culprit, or had she just had an accident?

Ruth's parents had been a handsome footman from the village and a dancer in a travelling circus that had passed through the valley eighteen years ago. They'd both been shooed out of town when she'd fallen pregnant without a ring on her finger, and her brother—Ruth's uncle—had followed them into the woods. When Hermana had first heard the story she'd thought it was romantic. Then she'd grown up. At best, both Ruth's father and her mother had been stunningly stupid, to think they could get away with having a child born out of wedlock in these parts. At worst, Ruth's father had been a rapist. Either way, they were both dead by the time Ruth had learned to walk; the woods were an unforgiving place.

The red-hot tip of the needle plunged down, and Hermana's teeth sank into her sock.

"Keep still, I said," Ruth scolded. "I'm almost done."

37

Keeping Hermana's earlobe pinched between forefinger and thumb, she plucked a tiny piece of gold from her pocket. Hermana winced as she felt the corpse's earring slide into her skin. There was a brief flare of pain which subsided into a dull throbbing, and there came a *click* as Ruth closed the latch.

Spitting out the sock and making a face at the taste it left behind, Hermana sat up and shook herself like a dog. Ruth held up a ladle she'd polished and let her examine her reflection.

"Hmm. Not bad, I s'pose."

"Bloody gorgeous, I'd say. Pretty as a picture."

Hermana covered her embarrassment by brushing a leaf from her hair and saying gruffly, "Not sure I like the sound of that. You said I'd look like a pirate. Pirates ain't pretty."

"Nah, I mean *it's* pretty. *You* look like a proper piece of scruff. Very pirate-ish."

"Oh. Right. Thanks."

Setting aside the ladle and pulling her to her feet, Ruth said, "Right. Let's go sort this out, then."

As they made their way up to the mushroom patch, Ruth said, "Do you ever want a baby?"

Hermana almost fell over. "You... *What*? God, no. A sprog? What would I do with it?"

Ruth shrugged. "I don't know. Forget it."

"Why'd you ask?"

"It's... All right, it's something Ned said. You know how, every now and then, he starts going on at me about how I should find myself a husband? Well, the last time he did, I asked him what good a husband would do me—to get him off my back, you see. He started rattling off this long list, things like money and respectability and what have you. And then he said that having a husband would mean I could have a baby. Like that was his trump card. When I told him I didn't want a baby, he looked at me like I was mad."

"Why? Babies smell. They're noisy. It's like...like keeping a chicken that doesn't lay eggs and that you can't eat." In fact, Hermana had nothing against babies—she wasn't entirely opposed to the prospect of acquiring one herself one day, provided she didn't have to do it the normal way—but she wanted to show Ruth that she was on her side. *To hell with you, Ned.*

"That's what I said. He wasn't having any of it. Kept going on about how I'd change my mind when I was an adult. I said I was an adult, I'm seventeen, and do you know what he said? He said you're not a proper adult until you've had sex."

This time, Hermana did fall over, astonishment causing her to miss an upraised root in her path. She scrabbled to her feet, sputtering incoherently.

"That was more or less my reaction," said Ruth. "So you do think he's wrong, then?"

"Of course he's wrong! What a stupid, *stupid* thing to say. Does he think all them fancy village girls are more adult than us, then? Those twits what haven't ever carried a bucket or climbed a tree or done a day's work in their silly lives—they all magically become adults as soon as some spotty boy gives them a quick going over behind a haystack? Bollocks."

Ruth nodded. "Right. Right. You're not in any rush to have sex yourself, then?"

Hermana was spared having to answer, or to ponder why she was being asked, by a sudden wave of utterly abominable stink.

"Oh my God," she groaned, clamping her hands over her nose. "That is *rotten.*"

"It's much stronger, isn't it?" Ruth agreed. "We're still a minute's walk from the patch."

By the time they reached the patch, Hermana's nostrils were stinging. By then, however, the smell was of little consequence compared to the sight that lay before them.

One of the things Hermana loved most about the mushroom patch was how mutable it was. The forest changed from season to season—black, skinny branches becoming thick, fruit-bearing boughs in summer; the river freezing over in the dead of winter; the spring thaw punctuated by the occasional rockslide blocking their usual pathways and forcing them to find new ways up the slope. The mushroom patch

39

changed from day to day. Every time they visited, it was a different world. There would be a new clump of fungus rising out of the remains of an old clump that had been healthy and abundant a week ago, new colours and textures and tastes, new insects. They'd had bees last year, a wasp nest two years ago, and before that there'd been a woodpecker, whose home had since been usurped by a family of squirrels.

But in all her seventeen years, Hermana had never seen anything like this. Half the mushrooms were dead, the Stubborn Duchesses, the King's Castles, and the delicate Angel Wings all collapsed into piles of greyish-black mush. The Big Bulls were still standing, but their thick stems were warped and their heads drooping, as though they were trying to grow back into the ground. What mushrooms remained were all stained with yellow flecks, and some, like the hardy Fat Ladies, had thin, web-shaped yellow lines stretching across their crowns. If Hermana stared at them for too long, it began to seem to her that they were pulsating.

The yellow muck had permeated every corner of the glade. Its tendrils touched the base of the Cod, and yellow spots were visible on the bark of all the surrounding trees. Beside the mushrooms, the wildflowers had withered and the weeds had shrunk to sad little wisps. Around the corpse itself, the rot had darkened to a burnt orange colour, with black streaks spread out beneath the body like tangled wings.

"Fuck," said Hermana.

Ruth looked as though she was about to cry.

Horrified, Hermana hastily added, "Here, Ruthie, it's not so bad. It's weird, that's all. As soon as we take care of the bastard, it'll all grow back in a week. You know what this place is like. Let's get it done, yeah?

Ruth pulled herself together and nodded.

"Yeah. I've had enough of this," she said, rubbing her palms into her eye sockets. "Bloody foreigner's ruined our patch."

An hour later, they stood back and examined their masterpiece. After several false starts, they'd settled for erecting a tall pyramid of sticks and leaves over their friend. It had taken them longer than it might have, as they'd decided not to pick up any fuel that had been contaminated. Conscious of the risk of the fire spreading out of their control, they'd cleared away all surrounding forest debris and then dug a moat around the pyre.

"It'll do," Ruth judged.

They drenched the whole thing in Ned's ungodly homebrew, a whiff of which was enough to make a man's nose hairs fall out. For a moment, it drowned out the stink of the yellow muck. Hermana got the fire going, and then they both sat back and patted one another on the back as they watched the blaze. It had been dry lately, and the wood burned fast. At its height, the fire rose twice as tall as Hermana. In lieu of a funeral hymn, Ruth sang a ballad Ned had learned from their mother, her voice low and scratchy, though she could carry a tune well enough. A light breeze picked up, scattering ash across the glade, and they both debated methods for concealing the smell of smoke when they got home.

As the fire began to die down, Hermana approached the remains of the pyre. "Well, I think that went all r— Oh."

Ruth said a rude word. In the centre of a circle of blackened earth and smouldering twigs, the corpse lay pristine.

Hermana touched its pale cheek and snatched her hand back. Shaken, she said, "Bastard's not even warm."

"This isn't right," Ruth said. "At least its hair should've burned."

The swaddle of cloth covering its hips had burned away, leaving it in a state of undress, but otherwise unmarred. They spent a few moments restoring its dignity with leaves.

"What if we piled dirt on top of it?" said Hermana. "A mound, sort of thing?"

"If it's not going to rot away, then eventually the dirt's going to slide off when it rains. Besides, I don't fancy knowing that he's here every time we come back, do you? How long is he going to keep stinking the place up? And making that yellow crap?"

After making sure the fire was out, they retreated down the slope in silence. Halfway to the bottom, Ruth stopped.

"I'm scared," she said, turning to look at Hermana. "Just realised it now. Are you?"

"A bit."

"You never look scared," said Ruth. "Even when we ran into that

41

bear, I remember you looked sort of angry and confused. You were scared, though, weren't you?"

Hermana nodded. She'd been terrified, as much by the bear as by the wild grin on Ruth's face as they'd run for their lives, and the way she'd laughed and whooped when they'd outpaced it and caught their breath. It had been the first time she'd realised that there were fundamental differences between herself and her best friend; up until then, she'd almost thought of them as one person with two bodies.

Ruth took her hand, her palm damp and warm. "These are our woods. No matter what the law says, or the village, or the fancy folk. They're *ours*. So we're going to sort this out. No mouldy old goblin's going to get the better of us."

With her jaw set and her eyes fire-bright and the single earring gleaming next to her face, she might have been a pirate queen. Hermana suddenly wanted to kiss her more than anything.

Instead, she nodded and said, "Let's make a new plan, then."

Chapter Seven

The first time Hermana had visited Ruth's house, Ned and Ruth's uncle had had a fight. As fists flew and a chair lost two of its legs in a shower of splinters, Ruth had pulled her under the table and instructed her to keep her head down. Later, after Ruth's uncle had stormed off to go stand on the crags overlooking the village and hurl curses at it—as was his wont when he was angry and sloshed—they'd helped Ned to his feet and cleaned the cut on his jaw.

"If you don't want to be friends anymore, I'll understand," Ruth had said when it was time for Hermana to go home, her shoulders set and her tiny chin tilted up with great and terrible dignity. "I'll spit on you because I'll be angry, but I'll understand."

The cut on Ned's jaw had become a scar, the edges of which had been softened by the intervening years. Ruth had once observed that it looked, from a certain angle, very much like a fat squirrel, and now that was all Hermana could see when she looked at it. It was deeply unfair, she thought. Wounds won in battle against fiendish adversaries three times your size should leave scars in the shape of swords or lightning bolts.

Hermana fixed her gaze upon Ned's scar while he and her grandmother debated the subject of the dirty river at dinner that evening, so as to avoid looking either one of them in the eyes. She was sure that one glance would be enough for them to know that she was keeping a secret.

"Never seen anything like it in my life," Ned told them. "I followed the river all the way up to the falls today—I didn't go any farther in case I ran into Mister Daniel's father or his men. It was the same no matter how far up I went; dead fish, sick birds, odd yellow film coating the water. I couldn't work out where it was coming from. It was like it was seeping out of the riverbanks. And it stinks to high heaven. I ended up going down to the village well to get water."

Maggie chewed her lip. "Maybe they're pouring something in—the fancy folk in their chalets. Some new type of soap. We'll have to start leaving tins out to catch rainwater."

"It's not only the water, though," Ned said. "While I was down in the village, I spoke to a few of old Cormire's farmhands. They said that they'd been seeing the same thing on the barley and the wheat; a sort of smelly, yellowish slime. They don't know what to make of it either."

Later, while the two of them were sharing a pipe and the girls were washing the dishes, Hermana whispered, "I've had an idea."

"What?"

"Salt."

"Salt? How's salt going to make the water drinkable?"

"No, no. I mean for our friend. Look, we're agreed that he's not a human, yes? He's something else, a goblin or an imp or something like that."

"Don't see what else he could be," Ruth conceded. "Although I'm still hard pressed to understand how he ended up in our mushroom patch. We've never had any silly occult nonsense in these woods before, whatever Gregor says about your gran."

"Right. Here's the thing; I remember reading this one book when I was a kid."

"You used to do a lot of reading," Ruth said, a hint of pique in her voice. While she'd never seemed to envy Hermana's literacy, she had made plain her resentment of the books that took up time Hermana might have spent in her company.

"I can't recall where I got it. I think it might have been one of Gran's. Anyway, it was about folklore and magic and all that twaddle. I remember they had a whole chapter on how to chase off evil spirits. I thought it was going to all about praying and not fiddling yourself—like the villagers say—but they kept going on about salt. You put a ring of it round your baby's cradle if you don't want him to be stolen by fairies. If you go to live in a new house, you throw some at the front door to make sure no ghosts follow you in. If you're travelling through the wilderness, you dab a bit on your ankles and toes so that sprites and other nasty things can't track you."

Fascinated, Ruth said, "Why? What don't they like about salt?"

"Hell if I know. Do you think it's worth a shot?"

"Pouring salt on him? Sure, why not? Can't hurt."

Their minds then turned to the vexing question of how to procure some. Salt was expensive in these parts of the world. Even when Ned could find work in the village, he rarely wasted his precious earnings on it, and though Maggie often brought home gifts and trinkets from her clients, she wouldn't keep salt in the house. She believed it was bad for the constitution.

In the end, there was only one place they could turn to.

✸✸✸

"It won't work," said Ruth, dropping the comb in disgust. "Your hair's hopeless. Never going to plait."

"Pigtail it then." Grimacing, Hermana hiked up her skirt and scratched her arse. "These knickers itch like hell."

"This frock's got moth eggs in it," Ruth commiserated as she squeezed Hermana's tight curls into two rigid pigtails. "God almighty, how do village girls do it?"

Their dresses had been gifts from Ruth's uncle, in one of his infrequent attempts to apologise to his niece for being a complete tosspot. They'd been much too big for them at the time, and now they were much too small for them. Hermana's dress had a great many pleats and a big, sagging bow at the back. It ended above her knees, showing off her hairy shins. Poor Ruth's was a sickly green and decorated with pictures of daisies. Having been made for a thirteen-year-old, its buttons were straining across her chest.

They'd washed their faces with morning dew, though their elbows and hands remained grimy and their fingernails quite unmentionable. Anyone who took a second look at them would know that they weren't proper village girls. But that was the thing about village girls; you weren't supposed to take second looks at them. Or first looks, if you could help it. Third and fourth looks were as good as declaring blood

45

feud upon their fathers, their brothers and three generations of their ancestors.

"What do we do if we run into Gregor?" Hermana asked.

"Leap into his arms and give him a big kiss," said Ruth. "Ned told me he's got a wife, and apparently she's pegged him for a philanderer. If word gets around that he's been philandering with the likes of us, she'll have his balls on toast."

Half an hour later, they stood together on the outskirts of the village.

Mar Reilly had once been at the spear tip of an expanding empire, thrusting deep into hitherto uncharted territory. Thanks to the valley's good soil and good weather, a thriving community had taken hold barely five years after it had been added to the map. Wealthy folk had followed, drawn by the promise of game, and the emperor had even commissioned a country residence to serve as his ninth holiday home. Then, for reasons unfathomable to the village's residents, its fortunes had changed. The empire had turned its attention eastward, where there were spices to be plundered. There was also the fact that the treacherous mountains surrounding Mar Reilly made it difficult to access, and its nearest neighbouring village was many miles away. Within a decade, the population had sunk to less than five hundred souls all told. Their most prominent contribution to the empire these days were exported pears; in honour of this distinction, one of the farmer's wives had embroidered a haloed pear onto the imperial flag that flew from the mayor's bathroom window.

Of the two of them, Hermana had visited the village most often, usually when Maggie's back was playing up and she needed someone to help carry her basket of ointments and potions. She had an idea of its layout, and which routes to take to avoid being spotted by the sheriff or one of Gregor's mates, who spent most of their days in or around the tavern. And she knew of one particular fancy house, with one particular window that was always left ajar so that the cook could pass leftovers and treats to the village's stray cats.

They held their breath as they snuck past the church and the mayor's house. No one stopped them or took any notice of them, and in short order, they were crouching below the window.

"Let's be quick," said Ruth, glancing over her shoulder.

Hermana nodded. She had vivid memories of the day, years ago, when they'd been caught nicking a sack of flour from the mill. Mercifully, neither of them had had tits at that stage, and Ruth's acne hadn't yet blossomed, so they'd been able to pass for ten-year-olds. If the farmhand who'd caught them had known they were both over twelve, he'd have been within his legal rights to take their index fingers. As it was, they'd escaped with a thrashing. It wasn't an experience Hermana cared to repeat.

Hermana kept watch while Ruth slid inside and slipped out a moment later bearing a large pot marked 'S'.

"Brilliant, Ruthie."

They'd had the perspicacity to bring along two clean handkerchiefs, into which they emptied half the pot's contents. They filled the rest with sand, and Ruth put it back where she'd found it.

"Where is everyone, d'you think?" asked Ruth as they crept away, their handkerchiefs full of salt safe in their pockets. "A place like this should be crawling with servants."

They received their answer as they made their way down the main road, taking the long way out of town so as not to retrace their steps, in case any of the villagers who had noticed them pass once already chose to ask what they were doing down here. It was market day. A dozen neat, sturdy stands lined the sides of the road, decorated with flags and hung with baskets of flowers. Servants wove in amongst the crowd, bearing parcels, packages, and harried expressions. Around each stand clustered five or six girls about their age, chatting and exclaiming over this beaded necklace or that little iced cake.

Hermana studied them with a lepidopterist's eye. They all had small waists, their hips emphasised by the cut of their colourful patterned skirts, and they all had on black buckled shoes, polished to a brilliant shine. Several of them wore jaunty summer hats with green ribbons tied to the brim. None of them wore their hair an inch below their shoulder lines.

Later, she couldn't recall what possessed her to reach out and swipe two of the ripest plums from the last stand as she and Ruth slunk by. Perhaps it was that she'd never tasted them before. Or perhaps it was that the handsome blonde girl with the smallest waist of all had looked at Ruth's dingy frock and smirked. Either way, no sooner had she slipped them into her pocket than a shout went up from behind them and a large hand wrapped around her wrist.

"Thief!"

She was yanked back so hard her arm was nearly pulled from its socket and then yanked in the opposite direction by someone who had caught hold of the back of her dress. A hand dove into her pocket, and the plums were drawn out, then held aloft by a matronly figure wearing a bonnet. As a cry of outrage went up through those assembled, Ruth tackled the man holding Hermana by the arm, only to find herself slapped across the face and taken hold of by two more market-goers.

"Get off!" she snarled, kicking and thrashing.

Hermana tried to bite the arm of one of her captors, as the stout shopkeeper she'd stolen from shouted at her, "You evil little robber! Touch my plums, will you?"

"Where do you missies get off, eh?" demanded another man. "This is a decent place!"

"Fetch the sheriff!" bellowed the bonneted matron, as Ruth and Hermana exchanged helpless looks.

"I know them," said the blonde girl. "They're the two who live in the woods. My mum told me about them. Have they really got black teeth?"

She leaned towards Hermana to get a better look, and Hermana let the wad of spit she had been rolling around in the back of her mouth fly. The girl shrieked as though it were acid, but retaliation never came, for at that moment the sheriff strode into view.

Tall and grave of feature, the sheriff wore a black buttoned shirt and a wide-brimmed black hat. As she had inherited the position and its budgetary constraints from her late father, both were a size too big.

"Please explain the state of affairs, sir," she said sternly to the shopkeeper, who recounted the theft in great excitement while Hermana and Ruth squirmed. The sheriff produced a notebook and scribbled in it as the two plums were presented for her inspection.

"I can't sell them now, not in good conscience," said the shopkeeper. "They've got that one's fingerprints all over them, look."

"I understand, Mr Truckle," said the sheriff, giving Hermana a stern frown. Though her face was not unattractive, she had a most forbidding nose. "I have assessed the situation, and I believe the appropriate recourse is an immediate flogging of the guilty parties."

A round of cheers went up.

"In the square!" shouted the blonde girl, and one of her friends added, "Someone fetch the cider, we'll make a party of it!"

The sheriff said, "Ladies, while justice must prevail at all costs, there is protocol to consider. The law prevents girls of their age being physically reprimanded in public. The flogging shall be carried out in the police station."

Taking Ruth's wrist in one hand and Hermana's in the other, the sheriff strode briskly towards an ugly brick building squeezed in next to the church, the crowd following at her heels. Someone threw an apple at them, which was retrieved and dusted off after the shopkeeper wailed about the damage being done to his merchandise.

Hermana was impressed by the older woman's strength. Their curses and kicks did nothing more than to provoke a ruffled sigh. They were dragged into the dusty confines of the police station, and the door was shut and locked behind them.

"Please do not make a fuss," the sheriff said, depositing them on a bench positioned in front of a small and tidy desk. The room had one cell and one window, barred and too high to see out of. There was also a second door, upon whose handle a well-maintained set of handcuffs were slung. "This will only take a moment."

Hermana could see Ruth calculating their chances of overpowering her and fighting their way out through the crowds. For her part, she had already given up and was trying to work out how they were going to explain the scars to Maggie and Ned. At least it didn't look like they were going to lose any fingers.

The sheriff took off her belt and whipped it through the air twice, making it sing. Raising her voice far louder than was necessary, she shouted, "Right, skirts up! Against the wall!"

49

Neither of them moved. From outside the police station there came a round of cheers and titters. Nodding to herself, the sheriff strode up to her desk and, drawing back her long arm, brought the belt down upon it. The resultant *crack* was greeted with more cheers and hoots of laughter from the crowd outside, and Hermana, catching on, screamed, "Aaargh! Oh, oh, please don't!"

Ruth looked at her like she was mad, while the sheriff brought the belt down a second time. On the third *crack*, Ruth worked it out, uttering a hideous shriek of pain. A lone voice in the crowd cried, "Oh, the poor dear!"

After twenty feigned blows, Hermana had to cram a hand in her mouth to keep from giggling, and Ruth came up with a loud, undignified squawking noise that was greeted by a hum of approval from the crowd. It sounded as though it was smaller now.

"You'll find they don't have much of an attention span," said the sheriff, returning her belt to her waist. She went to her desk and ferreted around in a drawer, taking out what smelled like a bacon sandwich wrapped in brown paper.

Placing it in Hermana's hands, she said, "My mother was sick when she was having me. I was too big, and I wouldn't come out properly. My father thought she'd die, so he sent for Miss Maggie, and she came all the way down the mountain in the dead of night. Safe to say that I was born more or less intact, my mother lived another ten years, and my family owes yours a great debt. Please take this. I'm sorry I don't have anything else. My salary is not substantial."

Hermana held the sandwich at arm's length. "Oh, I... Right. Um. "

"Thank you," said Ruth, taking it from her. "We'll tell Maggie you said hello."

"Tell her it's Joan Bailey, Stephanie Bailey's daughter. And...and give her this, would you?"

She took off her sheriff's hat and gave it to Hermana. "I can get another. I'd like her to know I've made something of myself. And I've got a son now, five years old. When he's bad, I tell him, 'Maggie Dim will come for you, mark my words'."

She gave them a sheepish grin, which Hermana returned, weakly.

50

Ruth took the hat and squinted at the lettering stitched in white thread across its front. Suspiciously, she said, "What's this say, then? 'Arrest us', or similar?"

Blinking, Joan began, "Oh, you can't re—" and then cut herself off. "It says 'Keeper of His Majesty's Law'. The numbers beneath are the date I was sworn in."

"Oh. That...well. Thanks. That's very... Thanks."

Feeling far more unsettled than they had been by the corpse, the two of them were quiet as they slipped out the back door to the police station and into the shelter of the trees.

After walking halfway home, they stopped and shared the sandwich, sitting back-to-back against an old oak, upon whose bark Hermana found two faint yellow spots. Hermana flipped the hat over, tried it on and then put it down, uncomfortable for reasons she couldn't articulate.

"We'll sneak back and leave it outside the station tomorrow," said Ruth, who could always tell what Hermana was thinking. Then she poked her in the ribs. "Why'd you never teach me letters? I felt like a right twit in there. You think I'm too stupid, is that it?"

"You run faster than me, you're taller than me, you catch fish and swim better than me, and you can dance. You don't have to be better at everything," Hermana retorted.

Besides, she thought, *if I taught you to read, Daniel would go from being annoying to being a problem. No nobleman alive would marry a woman who can't read.*

Chapter Eight

A basket full of stained linen sat at Mistress's feet like an offering to a heathen god.

"I find this sort of thing so disappointing," Mistress sighed and let the riding crop rest against her thigh.

Katie concentrated hard on keeping her gaze at exactly the right level—neither high enough to risk meeting her ladyship's eyes, nor low enough to keep her ladyship from seeing her face. The first would be indicative of insolence, and the second would suggest that she had something to hide.

"'M sorry, your ladyship," she mumbled. She had just returned from the marketplace and still carried the basket of cheeses and potatoes she had been instructed to purchase. The strap was beginning to cut into her shoulder. Shifting it to her other shoulder under Mistress's sad, unblinking gaze would have been impertinent. Putting it down on Mistress's cream-coloured carpet was unthinkable.

Mistress tilted her head to one side. "Sorry? I hardly see how it's your fault, my dear."

In her boots, the undersides of Katie's feet began to sweat. At her side, a small boy bit his thumb anxiously. His eyes were fixed on the riding crop; he was well acquainted with it.

Mistress smiled at him. She liked children. "How old is dear Charles now, Katherine?"

"Charlie's seven, Mistress. He's... He's not a bad boy."

Katie had to admit to herself that that was not strictly true. A servant's child who often fumbled his chores through carelessness and never bothered to express anything more than cursory repentance was, by definition, a bad child. The village priest was very clear on this point. Charlie was sweet-tempered and always willing to share his milk when

53

the other children asked nicely. But he was a touch slow and had not yet learned that those traits which suggested ideal moral character in civilised children did not count for very much when they flourished inexplicably within the younger brothers of servants.

"Charlie's very sorry too, my lady."

"Is he? I suppose that's something."

Katie had not witnessed Charlie's crime. Myrtle, an older maid, had relayed the sequence of events to her. That morning, Charlie had been asked to retrieve two fresh buckets of water for the laundry—the girl who usually saw to the task was complaining of bunions. Because he was frightened of the well and of all dark, empty spaces, he had gone down to the river to complete his chore. Distracted by his own thoughts, he had filled up the buckets without taking a good look at the water into which he was dipping them. He had then scampered back to the house whistling a tune, and had dumped both buckets of foul yellow slime into the tub containing Mistress's best linen.

Myrtle and the maids had done their best. They scrubbed until their fingers ached, but the stains wouldn't come out. Finally, they had surrendered to the inevitable and reported Charlie to the butler. They had given Katie apologetic looks as she was summoned to Mistress's study, which she had ignored.

"I was looking back through the records," said Mistress. She drew a slim book from the shelf on her right and opened it across her lap. "It looks as though this might not be the first *little problem* we've had with poor Charles."

Over the years, the Book of Little Problems had become as dreaded as any famous murderer amongst the household staff, as the list of names pencilled within its margins grew and grew. There was no escaping it. It remembered everything you did, forever, and the more times your name appeared in it, the worse each successive punishment would be. This was a trick Mistress had taken from pages of *The Modern House Manageress*, a popular twice-monthly pamphlet circulated throughout all the good houses situated at the outskirts of the empire. Mistress's copies often arrived late, allegedly because of the difficulties facing the Royal Mounted Post Service in obtaining access to the valley, and actually because every servant in the household hated the wretched things and were not above sneaking them from the mailbox and setting them alight. As soon as they arrived on her desk each one was read from front to cover, then placed beside its brothers on the shelf.

Katie's name had been written in the book two times, in all the years of her employment. Charlie's was on its seventh reiteration.

"Katherine, before we go any further, can I ask you to confirm for me your brother's complicity in this unfortunate business?" said Mistress.

Her pen hovered above the page. Katie, watching it, almost missed her cue. When the question and its ramifications filtered through, she glanced down at Charlie, now chewing his nails. Then she straightened her back. "Mistress, Charlie poured the dirty water into the tub."

Mistress sighed, and the pen started to descend like the blade of a guillotine.

"*After* I gave him the buckets," Katie continued. "I went down to the river, and I...I didn't see that the water was bad, I truly didn't. I wouldn't do that to your linen on purpose, Mistress. Only there was some young men lounging about on the riverbank. They whistled at me, so I wasn't paying proper attention to what I was doing. I'm sorry, Mistress."

Mistress squinted at her. "And Katherine, can you explain why you didn't go to the well to fetch the water?"

She swallowed and thought quickly. "Well, Mistress, the truth is I knew the men would be there. At the river. And I wanted them to whistle at me."

Mistress nodded, pityingly. "I see. Charles, you may go back downstairs."

"Thank you, Mistress," Katie murmured as he darted out the door.

"Against the bookcase, please, skirt up," said Mistress, making a mark next to Katie's name and getting to her feet. "I was your age once, Katherine. I do remember how thrilling it was to have the eye of a handsome young buck. But we mustn't let the side down."

"No, Mistress. We mustn't."

"We must maintain standards, mustn't we?"

"Yes, Mistress. We must."

55

"Thirty, I think."

"Yes, Mistress."

She lost count at ten.

That evening, Charlie helped rub ointment on her back, shame-faced and solemn.

"You're a very bad boy," she scolded, feeling cruel. But God alive, it *hurt*. "Next time you play silly games, Charlie, next time you don't take your chores seriously, I'm going to tell old Maggie Dim on you."

He whimpered.

Satisfied, she continued, "You know what's she like, don't you, Charlie? You know what I told you? She's three hundred years old, Charlie, and she's a proper savage, like the ones in books. Hair down to her ankles, her eyes all round and yellow. She's got *iron teeth*, Charlie. And you know what she *eats*?"

"'M sorry!" he squeaked and attempted to scuttle beneath the bed. She caught him and dragged him back.

"Oh, no you don't. You'll finish doing my ointment, thank you. And tomorrow, I'm going to ask Cook to think up some new chores for you. Seeing as you've got energy to daydream while you work, we might as well put that energy to use."

But she kissed his forehead when he curled up against her side in the late evening, and she accepted his third apology with grace.

❋❋❋

The salt didn't work.

"We've only used half of it," said Hermana forlornly. "Maybe it needs a bit more. Where's yours?"

"Hermie, it hasn't done *anything*," said Ruth, gesturing to the newly garnished corpse. "We've waited all day, and he doesn't look any more rotten than he did this morning. Besides, I don't want to waste mine on him. Been a long time since I've had salted potatoes. Come on, let's go home."

Hermana didn't argue. She had no desire to linger in the mushroom patch, which had only gotten weirder. The yellow rot had climbed halfway up the trees' trunks, and the surrounding dead foliage seemed...different. A large berry bush at one end of the glade had lost its leaves, and its branches were all twisted up, like gnarled old hands making fists. Glancing down, Hermana had spotted a beetle trundling through the muck, not dead like the others, but with extra legs and a head that seemed disproportionately large.

Halfway down the slope, they both jumped out of their skin at the sound of the gunshot. Hermana scowled as Daniel emerged through the trees with his blunderbuss and a pheasant slung over his shoulder. His tanned face was dappled with sweat, and he wore plainer clothes than normal, resembling a well-turned-out farmer's son, save for his expensive boots.

"Hello, lovelies," he hailed them.

"What're you up to, then?" said Ruth, eyeing the blunderbuss.

"Hunting, dear Ruth! Glorious day for it."

"You go chasing down the deer with that thing, soon enough they'll smarten up, and then we won't have a hope in hell of catching any with our arrows," Hermana told him curtly.

"Then you charming ladies shall have to come to me when you want venison," he smirked. "My cook does a wonderful roast. Hang on a tick, I've got something to show you."

Taking one of the pheasants in hand, he pushed back the feathers round its neck and showed them the yellow splotches beneath—thick buboes each as wide as a man's thumb. The flesh around them was red and inflamed, excepting those places where it had begun to turn black.

"Peculiar, isn't it? And it's all the over the place. My father's friends have reported the same phenomenon on the other side of the mountain. No one knows what's causing it. You know Lady Elizabeth Barnard? Well, no, you probably don't. She owns the chalet with the bright red roof. We found out yesterday that her white peacock's dead. Terrible shame, it was a lovely thing. *Very* expensive. We're considering sending for an expert from the capital. The problem is it takes letters such a damned long time to reach them."

"Daniel," Ruth said, her voice low and insistent. "You're going to wash your hands, yeah? Soon as you get back home? And don't eat that pheasant, it..."

57

"My *word*. Are you concerned for me, sweet Ruth?" For a brief moment, he looked bashful. "Don't worry. One of the apiarists fell ill on Tuesday, yellow spots all up her arms and neck. We've been taking precautions since then. Father never travels this far from civilisation without his personal physician, and I know how to take care of myself. I do worry for you, though. I brought this."

He reached into the bag hanging at his side and withdrew a small jar.

"What are they?" said Ruth, taking off the lid and plucking out one of the wrinkled, orange objects therein.

"Peaches. Dried and preserved, they'll keep for weeks. Marvellous for the constitution."

Ruth gave him *that* smile, the one Hermana had always thought was for her alone. "Thank you, Danny. That's...that's nice of you."

"How much did they cost, then?" Hermana asked.

Blinking, Daniel replied, "I...er, I don't know. The butler arranges these things. Listen, I should be getting back. Ruth—don't forget your promise."

"The foal, right. I'll come and see it soon."

"I'll hold you to that!" he called over his shoulder and strode away, whistling.

"Those things look like week-old brains what's been scooped out of a rabbit's head," Hermana told her. "I'd leave them alone. Might give you wind."

"Why've you always got to be so nasty to him?" Ruth complained, stuffing one into her mouth. "He never did you any harm in his life."

"He's...he's...he's rich. I don't trust rich folks."

"You don't trust poor folks, either, or folks in the middle. You always treat him like he trod on your toes and laughed about it. It's not fair to him."

"What's it matter? He doesn't care one way or the other how I treat him. You're the one he's interested in."

"Fucking hell, Dim, don't tell me you're *jealous*."

Hermana tried to think of a response and couldn't.

"You want him to leave *you* flowers, is that it?" said Ruth, her voice

58

growing strident. "You want him to give you peaches and call you 'my dear'? Well, I can tell you right now, that's not ever going to happen if you keep being a complete bitch to him."

The argument may well have escalated, had they not arrived at Ruth's house just then and seen Ned outside chopping firewood. His shirt was off, and there were yellow spots all over his arms.

Chapter Nine

"Ruth, wait," Hermana said the next day.

"Shut your mouth, Dim," Ruth told her and hefted the axe higher.

Ned hadn't noticed the spots until they were pointed out to him. He'd been more curious than alarmed, and he'd told them not to worry.

"I'm a big strong boy," he said, ruffling Ruth's hair. "I've shaken off worse than this."

But when Ruth had brought him his supper later that evening, he'd had no appetite. He'd gone to bed early and woken up in the middle of the night soaked with sweat and complaining of cramp in his stomach. Then the retching had started.

Ruth had arrived at Hermana's door in panic three hours before dawn, and together they'd woken up Maggie. As Hermana's grandmother tended to Ruth's brother, the two of them had paced back and forth for hours and then sat down in a corner together with their hands tightly clenched, like when they were children.

At midmorning, Maggie had asked for tea and told them that she thought the worst was over. Ruth had thrown her arms around her and kissed her cheek a dozen times.

When she'd turned to Hermana, though, her eyes had been bright with rage. When she'd stormed outside and picked up the axe, Hermana had worried that she'd gone mad.

"We've tried everything else," Ruth said now, standing over the corpse. "I don't like it any more than you do—it'll be a mucky business, no doubt. But the bugger's got to go, even if we have to bury him in bits."

The axe went up. The axe came down. The axe was flung across the glade, and Hermana sighed as her friend set about giving the corpse a damn good kicking.

"Not a scratch," panted Ruth, when she had calmed down. "*Fuck.* I hit him right in the gut. Look, nothing. It's like he's made of iron."

Hermana hunkered down and pressed the palm of her hand against his cheek. Granules of salt from their last effort still coated his skin, and they stuck to her hand as she drew it back. "He's still so soft, though. Maybe—"

She cut herself off. She had unusually good hearing—Maggie said she got it from her—and she could just discern the sound of approaching footsteps.

"I think someone's coming," she whispered to Ruth.

"Here?" Ruth said, looking incredulous. "No one ever comes here except us."

"Let's hide," said Hermana. The footsteps were definitely not those of an animal. She was entertaining a notion that whoever had murdered their goblin had finally come back to clean up after themselves.

They concealed themselves behind one of the dead trees. A moment later, someone stepped into the glade.

They both knew better than to gasp, though Ruth's arm—which had found its way around Hermana's shoulders—did tense up. The woman was tall, taller than the sheriff, and naked save for a loincloth and a string of grey beads around her neck. Her shoulders were wide and brawny, an archer's shoulders, and the flanks of her legs were packed thick with muscle. Long, pale hair cascaded down her shoulders, shining as though coated with silver dust, and gold rings pierced her navel, her nipples, and her ears. Her green, pointy ears.

Hermana was not oblivious to the fact that she was strikingly beautiful, even more so than the corpse. She couldn't resist leaning out just a few more inches from behind the shelter of the tree, to get a better look, and as soon as she did, she heard a twig crack under her foot.

She ducked back immediately, and Ruth scowled at her. They both waited in silence, crouching low, until they heard the woman speak. Her voice was rough, and her tongue was foreign, but it sounded like an order. The girls exchanged looks and then stepped out into the glade.

Hermana blinked. "What the hell?"

The woman's skin was no longer green. Her ears were no longer pointy. Though she was still mostly naked, in all other respects, she looked like a normal human woman of about twenty-five years of age.

"Ooh, that's clever," murmured Ruth.

The woman was looking at them with fear doing its best to hide behind anger. She spoke again, pointing to the body.

"We...we can't understand you," said Hermana. She took a cautious step forward. "Where did you come from?"

"Idiot. What makes you think she can understand *you*?" said Ruth.

"She's a fucking goblin. Who knows what she can do?" Hermana hissed.

The woman was running her eyes over them, some of her obvious fear having abated. She seemed particularly preoccupied with their feet.

"We found him," Hermana continued. "We've been trying to bury him. I'm Hermana Dim, and this is Ruth Honeyduck. Do you have a name?"

The woman said a word with about twenty syllables, most of which Hermana didn't think she could pronounce.

"Um. Great. It's nice to meet you," she said, offering out her hand.

The woman stared at it for a moment and then tentatively took it. A second later she yelped and snatched her arm back.

"Hermie, look!" Ruth said, pointing. All up the woman's arm, the pink-peach colour was disappearing and the pale green was coming back. "What did you do?"

"I think... I think it was the salt," Hermana said, staring at her own palm. "Some of it came off and—"

Before she could say another word, the woman snarled at them and ran.

Ruth swore. "Come on! We need to catch her!"

"What? Why?"

"She might be our last chance," Ruth called back, already outdistancing her.

"Oh God." Hermana groaned and followed after her.

The two of them knew every inhabitant of the forest, fanged and feathered and legless. Ruth could smell the difference between red deer crap and reindeer crap. Hermana could identify thirty-two different varieties of bird footprint. They'd hunted rabbit, boar, weasel, fox, pheasants—anything that had meat on its bones.

The woman ran like nothing they'd ever known. In minutes, they'd lost her, and they couldn't find any tracks.

"How does someone that big not leave tracks?" Ruth said.

While Ruth had her nose to the ground, Hermana was hopping with excitement. "Ruth, we've found a living one! Hell, I wonder if there's more. Maybe there's whole village of them living somewhere in these woods!"

"Don't be stupid. How could we have missed a whole village of goblins?" said Ruth. "Ah! What's this?"

She'd found a trail of tiny flowers, with petals a dazzling array of reds, blues, oranges. They grew in little clumps, divided by a couple of paces, and Hermana realised that they were arranged in the shape of footprints, proceeding into the distance.

"Flowers grow where she walks. That's useful," mused Ruth.

They followed the flower tracks for half a mile, until they reached the dark rocks that lined the river's banks. The smell from the contaminated water was so strong that neither of them could bear to go on.

"*Damn.* How're we going to find her now? If she can disguise herself as a human she can go anywhere. Maybe she can even disguise herself as mole or a bear," said Ruth. "God, did you see her tits? Why does anyone need tits *that* size?"

"No wonder she goes about starkers. Probably isn't enough fabric in all the world," said Hermana. "Look, maybe she's going to take care of our friend for us. We might come back tomorrow and find that he's gone."

They discussed their strange visitor all the way back down the slope, speculating as to where she'd come from, what else she could do, how she was related to their corpse. They made plans to return to the glade at noon the next day.

When Ruth got home, her brother was dead.

Chapter Ten

Five days later, Hermana's grandmother laced up her boots, picked up her bow, and strode out into the morning mist. The dawn chorus assailed her ears as she slipped between the trees, her nostrils twitching at the funny smell that had permeated the woods for the last few days.

Odd, that. Don't like it. Don't like it at all. Feels wrong, like someone's up to mischief.

Hermana was at Ruth's house, having stayed there since the funeral. Not many people had come. Maggie, the two girls, and three of Ned's drinking mates from down in the village. One of them, Freddie, had brought a fistful of daisies and six copper coins, placing both into Ruth's hands in payment for an old debt he'd owed her brother. They'd not had a priest—he wouldn't have come this deep into the woods. Afterwards, Maggie had tried to convince Ruth to come and stay with her, but she'd refused to leave her brother's house. Hermana had remained behind instead.

Maggie suspected that the decent thing for her to do would have been to stay behind as well, to help Ruth tidy up and burn the bed Ned had died on. She had, at least, cleaned away the residue of those final, awful hours while the girls had been off in the woods and she'd been alone with him—the blood, the vomit, the sticky yellow pus that had begun to trickle from his ears.

It was so quick. I thought he was on the mend. I told them he was on the mend, just hours before...

Yes, she should have stayed with Ruth. But Maggie knew herself for a coward. She didn't want to have to meet her granddaughter's accusing gaze, and moreover, the thought of spending even a night away from her own house filled her with horror. What if she came back and someone had taken it, like they'd taken the cabbages and three of the chickens last

65

winter? Her worries were not unfounded; a great many things had been taken from Maggie Dim over the course of her long, long life.

Enough moping, she told herself. She'd catch the girls something nice for supper. A pheasant or a partridge or...

There. From behind a gooseberry bush, a flash of brown; a female deer, two years old. Maggie's reflexes were faster than most women her age. Even so, she didn't hold out much hope as she drew the arrow back. Her mind was ill at ease, and it hurt her aim. At best, she hoped to graze it.

She was startled when the arrow landed dead centre of its chest.

A moment later, she crouched over her kill. *Not right. It heard me, I'm sure of it. Why was it so slow to get away?*

Her fingers traced the yellow splotches that spotted its long neck, its muzzle and its belly.

"Oh!"

Maggie lifted her head to see that a small, plainly dressed woman had stepped out from behind a row of ash trees and stood frozen, her eyes glued to the dead deer.

"Oh," she said again and then, "Oh, goodness."

She put a hand over her mouth, bending at the waist as though to retch. Maggie watched her, noting the basket she carried over her shoulder and the neat and inexpensive little bonnet. A servant, she deduced, most likely delivering something to the fancy folk who lived by the falls.

"What d'you want?" she barked. It wouldn't do for any representative of the village to feel that they were welcome in her territory.

"I...I do apologise. I got lost—I'm not familiar with these woods. I was trying to find my way back to the road. Please, don't let me bother you, Missus Dim. I'll go this way..."

The servant made to retreat behind the trees once more, when they were both distracted by a squelching noise coming from the deer's corpse.

Maggie stood quickly and stepped away from it. She and the servant watched, transfixed, as the dead deer's flesh began to ripple. The yellow spots were *moving*, stretching and slithering across its hide like worms, then clumping together and turning black. Soon, the deer was covered in a collection of large, quivering black lumps. The skin around its mouth melted away, revealing another lump upon its lolling tongue, and its legs twitched as though it still harboured ambitions of escaping the arrow.

Something that Maggie could only describe as a sprout emerged out of the largest of the lumps. It grew to a height of five feet in half a minute, and soon it loomed over them both its stem waving from side to side in the breeze. Sickeningly pink petals burst forth from its tip and spread out until the flowers were as broad as dish plates.

Then the plant bent, as though it were a man stooping to pick up a dropped coin. It came level with the girl's face.

"Missus Dim," she whispered. "What should I..."

From within the depth of the petals a lump of tar shot forth like a cannon ball. Some of it covered the girl's eyes and cheeks, but the greater portion landed squarely at the back of her mouth, where it began to choke her.

She collapsed to the ground, writhing, clawing at her throat as she tried to cough it out. Without taking her eyes off the flower, Maggie got hold of her by the shoulders and dragged her away from it. Then she took hold of the smaller woman's jaw and shoved her long fingers past her teeth.

She drew them back, clutching a ball of tar and drenched in saliva, the woman hacked and gagged, rolling onto her front as she coughed up residual strings of filth.

Five minutes later, they sat together with their backs to a large oak, recovering. They'd put several more metres and half a dozen trees between themselves and the plant, though they could still hear the squelching noise coming from the deer's corpse.

"Thank you," said the girl, her voice faint and raspy.

Maggie grunted, wiping her hand off on her shirt. "What's your name, girl?"

"Katherine Bellows, ma'am. I work for Lady Dorothy Piper."

"That diabolical bitch? Pity. How long've you had to put up with her?"

"I'm not sure, exactly. I've served Lady Piper since I was a child, and I'm twenty-three now."

"Really? You look older. I've got a granddaughter only a few years younger than you."

"Yes, I've...I've met her a few times. Missus Dim, do you know what thing that was?"

"Predatory and unnatural. Beyond that, your guess is as good as mine, dear."

Katherine glanced back through the trees, seeming to make sure it hadn't sprouted legs and followed them. "The yellow spots on its hide—I've seen them before. They're all over the wheat and the barley, and the pear trees too. People say it's the same stuff that's gotten into the river."

"Makes sense, I suppose."

"The priest is saying it's a punishment."

"You agree with him?"

People probably did not ask for Katherine's opinion. She was silent for a moment.

"You think there's enough wickedness in your village for God to inflict this sort of thing on you?" Maggie prompted.

Katherine said slowly, "If I was God, and I could do *anything*, I wouldn't punish us like this, in a way that hurts the good folks as much as the bad. I'd go after the bad ones directly—give one a horrible disease, make another one fall down a ladder, and another one burn alive. That would be much more efficient."

Maggie raised an eyebrow. "You'd make a great and terrible God, Miss Bellows."

They shook hands, and Maggie directed her back to the road.

Chapter Eleven

The sheriff was trying to fix the well.

Progress was slow. While Joan Bailey had many fine qualities, an understanding of windlasses and water tables was not among them. Ordinarily, the task would have fallen to the baker's son, who served as the town's handyman. When she'd knocked on his door, his wife had informed her that he was sick, on account of having been one of the unlucky ones to have drunk from the well before anyone noticed the foul stink pouring out of it. Nine other members of the community were reporting ill relatives.

Joan's hope was that a dead bird had fallen in. She wasn't optimistic; the smell arising from the blackness below was exactly like the one coming from the river.

Peering into the well's depths, she almost missed the approach of Katie Bellows. This, for Joan, would have been highly unusual. As she had long since memorised the sound the small woman's buckled shoes made when they fell upon the cobblestones, she glanced up at the last minute.

"Good day, Miss Bellows," she said, tipping her hat.

Katie blinked up at her, swallowing. "Good day, Sheriff."

Joan took in her round, wet eyes, the grass and soil staining her skirt, and the dishevelled state of her bonnet. "Miss Bellows, I hope you will not mind my asking: Is everything—"

"Katie-girl! Aren't you looking lovely today?"

Joan closed her eyes and prayed for patience.

Gregor leaned against the side of the well, his bristled face beaming. Since Joan's trusted deputy had fallen ill, he had volunteered to serve in his place. There were many, many young men who Joan would have preferred to Gregor, and as luck would have it, they were all busy nursing sick relations or out in the fields trying to salvage the crops. And Gregor had, at least, seemed eager, informing her that he had always wanted to be a lawman when he was younger.

"Nothing I like better than nicking felons," he had said and glanced towards Joan's jailhouse in a way that suggested that its emptiness was less indicative of an orderly, law-abiding community, and more of a sheriff shirking their duties. Joan had refrained from pointing out that many of Gregor's drinking mates were foremost among those citizens who did make frequent visits to her cell.

As deputy, his main contribution thus far had been to stick his head down the well, sniff, and proclaim, "She's buggered, Joan, and no mistake."

"Hello, Mister Markbridge," said Katie.

"Been walking, have we?" he asked, something in his tone making the question salacious. "That's good to hear! Puts a rosy flush on your cheeks, walking does. I always did approve of a healthy girl."

"Thank you, sir," Katie mumbled.

"You walk a lot, do you?"

"No, sir. Only when I'm told to."

"Well, I like a nice walk myself, as it happens. Nothing better, far as I'm concerned. Maybe next time Lady Piper's got an errand for you, we can walk together."

"That would be lovely, sir. Goodbye."

"Are you sure you're all right, Miss Bellows?" asked Joan, as she began to move off.

Gregor clicked his tongue. "Honestly, Bailey, stop pestering the girl!"

When Katie was out of earshot, he whispered in Joan's ear, "She's not bad, eh?"

Not for the first time, Joan mulled over the question of whether her life was made easier or more challenging by the fact that most of the people she knew spoke to her as though she were a man.

Oblivious to her silence, Gregor continued, "There's something about girls like her, isn't there? It's the hips, I think. You don't see hips like that on women who don't have a few drops of native blood in them.

70

Mind you, you're a bit of a... Well. You know. Bit of a mystery yourself."

"If you're referring to my grandfather, Mister Markbridge, you should be aware that he was from the far north. Miss Bellow's heritage is of the western grassland tribes, and I do not think her hips are any business of ours."

Gregor shrugged. "As you say, Sheriff. Not our business. A bit of skirt's a bit of skirt as far as I'm concerned. I'm not a bigot, myself... I hate everyone equally!"

And he grinned, as though this were the apex of wit.

Joan considered a range of responses, before settling on, "Mister Markbridge, as my deputy, would you perform a small chore for me? Would you climb down into the well and ensure that there are no dead animals floating in it?"

Gregor paled. "Me? Climb into *that*?"

"Mm. Indeed. While you're down there, you can inspect the water and see if its state is similar to that of the river."

Gregor glanced down into the dark, stinking depths. "Right. Right. Good plan. Here's a thought, though—what if we got that gardener of Lady Piper's to go down instead? Fred, that's his name. He's scrawnier than me. Less likely to get stuck."

Joan patted his shoulder. "Gregor, I couldn't possibly entrust a task as important as this to a mere servant. The health and safety of the whole village is at stake. I'm sure you'll be fine. If you *do* get stuck, try not to breathe in. Prolonged exposure to the fumes might make you very ill."

She kept a watchful eye as he lowered himself in, and then she went off to do other things.

71

Chapter Twelve

Hermana had come to accept that she was crap at giving comfort. She just didn't have the knack. Everything she said came out sounding forced or stupid. So when the sun rose six days after Ned's death, and Ruth still lay on his bed, staring blankly up at the ceiling, Hermana went to fetch Daniel.

When she followed the path up to the chalets, something went wrong.

In years gone by, she and Ruth had often bartered with travellers who had gotten lost in their woods, exchanging directions for small items of food or clothing. When she was younger, Hermana had assumed that they were all idiots. The woods weren't *that* big. How could anyone with a lick of sense not be able to find their way out? Since then, she had come to realise that people who lived their lives surrounded by buildings had an entirely different way of looking at things. They saw no difference between a line of rough-barked conifers with an uneven row of smooth beech trees. They missed all the telltale landmarks—the woodpecker, the strawberry bush, the pile of boar crap. Living in a town made their brains too brittle to navigate their way through anything that wasn't a town.

Knowing that had always given Hermana a smug glow of superiority. So it was with extreme disconcertion and annoyance that she found herself totally lost.

The smell and the yellow slime coating several of the trees was distracting, but that wasn't all it was. The woods seemed to be playing with her. The rocky outcropping shaped like a tortoise had gone, or she'd missed it. The sycamores were at least thirty metres from the spot where she'd expected to find them, and both of them were leaning the wrong way, forcing her to wonder if they were not two entirely different

73

sycamores that she had never noticed before.

"Stop mucking about," she said aloud, in the voice Maggie used when her pet pig was making a nuisance of itself.

Every few steps, something seemed to slither or hiss behind her. Once, a fluttering noise came from the shadows on her left; it sounded about the right size for a partridge, though the image that immediately came to her mind was of giant fibrous moth wings, not feathers. Of course, when she looked, there was nothing there.

"I'm not in the mood for playing games," she told the woods under her breath. "I know you've been out of sorts of late. We've been doing our best to fix it."

As she passed by the larger patches of yellow muck, several of them flickered as though reflecting light from a candle that she definitely wasn't carrying.

"That's a new trick," she muttered, to stave off the urge to piss herself. *Bugger, when did it get so cold?*

She wasn't certain she was going in a straight line. Every time she tried to reach a target, a clump of weeds or a tree, something wriggled in the corner of her vision, distracting her. When she looked ahead again, the path was subtly different, although she couldn't say quite how.

Shutting her eyes, she said, "I don't know how you're doing this, Mister Dead Goblin—or maybe it's Mrs Alive Goblin. Whichever it is, you should know that I've been here a lot longer than you have. When we were kids, me and Ruth used to play a game where we'd climb up the slope with our eyes closed, and see who made it to the top first. I was always the winner."

She kept still for a moment and then turned on her heel, her eyes still closed. She walked forward with slow, even steps. When something shuffled through the trees to her right, she neither stopped nor picked up the pace. When she seemed to tread on the same pebble twice in the same minute, she kept walking in a straight line. After a few minutes, the strange noises died away. She kept her eyes closed nonetheless, until...

"I say, are you all right?"

Blinking, she looked up to see Daniel standing right in front of her, his expression concerned. Before answering him, she looked around and saw that she was back on the path to the chalets. She let out the breath she'd been holding and placed a hand on his shoulder to check that he was solid.

"Whole fucking forest's gone mad," she said, mostly to herself.

"There, there," said Daniel, visibly discomforted by her proximity. "Come now, tell me what's wrong. Where's Ruth?"

As they made their way to Ruth's house, Daniel chattered amiably while Hermana maintained a stony silence.

"Did you know that there are tribes in the Far East that believe that the first sign of the apocalypse will be a great dying off of flora and fauna? Their gods made the plants and animals first, you see, and it's assumed that they'll unmake everything in the same order. The last man alive would be left floating in a black void before the gods unmade him."

Hermana pretended to be too busy chewing her thumbnail to reply.

"This has all gotten a bit out of control, hasn't it?" said Daniel a few moments later, after sidestepping a stinking patch of muck. "Father's decided it's time to bring in the experts. Yesterday he sent a letter to a professor of biology in the capital. God only knows how long it'll take to reach him, the postal service being what it is. Of course, I took a few biology courses at the academy. Not much use to me now, I'm afraid. To be honest, I spent most of my time playing jacks with the chaps at the back of the hall."

A thought occurring to her, Hermana asked, "Did they ever have a course on goblins at your academy?

"Goblins? Hmm, not as such. I do remember a friend of mine who spent a year writing a dissertation titled 'The Legends and Mythologies of Primitives Cultures'. He said..."

"You believe in them?"

"What? Believe in goblins? Well, no. Of course I don't."

He chuckled; then, after he noticed her face, he added, "I mean, it's fine if *you* do. Everyone should believe in something. It's quite a charming thought, really."

"Right, thanks," said Hermana, and she ignored him for the rest of the journey.

Ruth was waiting outside the house when they arrived. Daniel knelt and kissed her hand. "Dear, sweet Ruth. Words cannot express... What a loss. What a fine man he was. We are all worse off without him."

"Danny," she replied, her voice raspy from disuse. "What're you doing here?"

"I'd like to pay my respects, Ruth."

"I see. All right."

They took him to the grave. Ned had been buried beside one of their favourite trees; they called it Old Grim. It had been one of their first secret hiding spots, before they'd grown too big to climb its topmost branches. Maggie had said that Old Grim was nine hundred years old and that he used to be a hanging tree, which had only made them love him all the more.

Looking closely, Hermana saw that Old Grim's knotty roots were flecked with yellow spots. As Daniel knelt at the grave with his hands clasped, she tried to pick some of the infected bark off with her fingernails.

When Daniel was done mumbling, Ruth said, "That was a proper prayer, wasn't it? Same language the village priest uses at weddings and whatnot."

"That's right," said Daniel, smiling. "It's the language of the church. Father made me spend three years becoming fluent."

"Not bad," said Hermana, doing her best to be gracious. "You need lots of brains to hold two languages in your head."

Daniel took out his expensive knife and began carving letters into Old Grim's trunk. When he was done, he said, "There. I think that would please him."

"I can't read it," muttered Ruth, and something in Hermana twisted.

"It says, 'Here rest the mortal remains of Edward Honeyduck, beloved brother and son'."

Ruth looked thoughtful. "Well, I don't know about that. I don't think either Mum or Dad gave a shit about either of us. But you're right. He'd have liked it. Hermie, you add something."

Taking Daniel's proffered knife, Hermana carved another row of

76

letters underneath his neat block capitals:

he wOss tRRifec

Ruth nodded in approval. "Looks good."

Daniel kissed Ruth's hand again before he left, and she hugged him tight.

"I'm hungry," Ruth announced as they headed away from Ned's grave. "Let's go find some eggs."

Relief washed over Hermana. Ruth hadn't eaten more than few mouthfuls of porridge for days, much less displayed any interest in going foraging. "Good idea."

Her good mood held strong even after two hours of hunting, during which all the nests they found were either empty or contained eggs that were rotten.

"We might have the rest of Daniel's peaches lying around somewhere," said Hermana, climbing down a tall oak, careful to avoid the yellow patches. Because she was feeling charitably inclined towards the nobleman, she added, "Nice of him to bring us those, even if they do look a bit weird. After all, fancy folk have a thing for weird food, don't they? Swans' feet and spicy crickets in gravy, that sort of thing. The more foreign and awful it is, the more they pay for it. Who knows how much those peaches cost? It..."

Ruth, who had been standing watching her with a contemplative expression, suddenly stepped forward and pushed her back against the tree's trunk. Then Ruth kissed her.

An odd thing happened at that moment. All Hermana's senses became far more acute. She could smell all the thin layers of sweat, dust, and soil coating Ruth's skin, and the hot meat beneath it. She could hear the footsteps and slitherings of every animal that moved within a mile. She could feel Ruth's taste buds as though they were large rocks growing out of her tongue, and the slight gap between her two frontmost upper incisors as though it were a canyon.

Hermana jerked back and kicked her shin.

"Right, let's go find those peaches, then," she said as Ruth clutched her leg. She started walking briskly downwards, and after a moment,

Ruth caught up with her.

Upon returning home, they located the peaches, ate them, and pretended as though nothing had happened.

Chapter Thirteen

The mayor had called an emergency meeting in the square.

The crowd gathered before him was not as large as it might have been. Everyone who arrived had come either without or in lieu of a relative or a friend. Most of those who were absent had fallen sick after drinking from the river or eating a tainted berry. But not all of them, that was the worst part. Some had slept beside a lover who was sick. Some didn't seem to have caught it from anything; they just woke up covered in pale yellow spots. The illness—if it *was* an illness, no one had even come to an agreement on that yet—seemed to have no defining characteristics. Once the spots appeared, its victims might come down with any conceivable symptoms, from nausea to buboes to fever. Farmer Grey's ninety-year-old mother had spent a whole day vomiting up every morsel of food that touched her lips, while yellow spots erupted all over her face. The next day, she'd been out of bed and helping her son clean the linen. Concomitantly, Mrs Bligh's hearty young son had complained of a rash and a queasy feeling and had died within five hours.

"All food found to have gone bad is to be discarded and buried," the mayor announced. "Anyone showing signs of infection is to report directly to the physic and the priest. The clothes of the infected are to be burned. No one is to drink from the river under any circumstances, nor swim in the river, nor..."

Katie stood at the back of the crowd, trying to remain inconspicuous. Of late, she and the other servants had been the recipients of many a harsh look and sideways glance when they went about their business in the streets. There were rumours that Lady Piper and the village's other wealthy residents were secretly stockpiling food. Now that more than half the crops were tainted, food was all anyone seemed to talk about.

Katie didn't know if the rumour was true. She certainly hadn't seen anyone sneaking bags of grain and vegetables into the house. Lady Piper seemed immune to the slow panic gripping her neighbours.

After all, it's not as though she's at risk of starving, Katie thought. *If things get much worse, she'll just take her carriage and go to stay with her relatives in the capital.*

Yesterday, for the first time in her life, Katie had stolen. She'd waited until dinner, when everyone was busy serving or helping Cook, and had complained of dizziness. No one had questioned her, and no one had noticed her sneaking off to the cellar and detracting two bottles of wine.

Water, she'd thought, carrying them back to her room. *That will be the first problem.*

Though few people would have suspected it of her, Katie had a vivid imagination. Inside her head, she was painting a picture. As people abandoned the river, the well, and the as-yet-uncontaminated springs, it would be the animals that would die first—the cattle, the pigs, and finally the pets. The mayor had already advised them all to start collecting rainwater, but everyone was expecting a dry year. The tavern keeper would begin hoarding his liquor. Those who could leave, would. Eventually, the mayor would implement a rationing scheme, and they would have to queue for food and water. Representatives of the fancy folk's houses would be at the front of those queues, with the mayor and the priest behind them, and then the baker and the carpenter and the dressmaker, and all their wives and children. Katie would have to take her place at the back of a hundred people to get her share. Only, of course, she wouldn't, because waiting in a line that long would mean she wouldn't be able to finish all her chores for the day. Which would mean a beating. Which would mean she would need extra water to clean the wounds.

I am a thief, she'd thought as she'd hidden the bottles under her bed. If she was found out, it wouldn't be the cane, or the whip. They'd brand her.

While Charlie had eaten his breakfast, she'd checked him all over for spots. Finding none, she'd instructed him not to eat or drink

80

anything she hadn't inspected first.

"Why not?" he'd asked, his mouth full.

She'd waved a finger in his face. "Because if you do, I'll tell Maggie Dim. You know what she does to little boys who don't listen to their sisters?"

He'd swallowed what was in his mouth without chewing and promised to do as he was told. Recalling the crotchety old woman who'd saved her from the flower, Katie had smiled to herself and wondered if she might get a chance to introduce them one day.

A handful of farmers had come to stand alongside the mayor. One by one, they relayed the states of their crops; more than half the barley contaminated, almost all the wheat beyond hope, thirty-five percent of the pear trees dead. Ten sickly cattle and seven dead ones; three dead goats; twenty-six dead chickens. The pigs, strangely enough, seemed immune.

In amongst the crowd, theories were exchanged in whispers.

"I spoke to the schoolmaster," said the baker's wife. "He says the village was built over an ancient piece of native territory, one of those places where they used to perform their ghastly ceremonies."

"Oh, so we're being cursed by savage gods, is that the idea? Nonsense and poppycock," said the tavern keeper's aunt. "If they existed, they would have seen us off when we first settled in."

"The priest says it's because people have been having too much...um, too many nocturnal activities. Activities of a fleshly nature, I mean," said the mayor's oldest daughter, blushing.

"That again? He's always on about that. It hardly seems fair anymore. We do our best, but you've got to make children *somehow*."

"I think the priest's point is more that people are engaging in the wrong *sort* of nocturnal activities," said the baker's wife.

The tavern keeper's aunt looked blank. "How many sorts are there? I can only think of two. Maybe three, depending on semantics."

As they embarked on a spirited discussion as to the varieties of nocturnal activities and their relative sinfulness, Katie slipped away. As she did, she passed by a tall woman with long hair and broad shoulders standing at the edge of the crowd and observing the assembly with the sort of interest adders reserved for field mice. Katie didn't recognise her and assumed that she must've been a travelling merchant or perhaps a servant in one of the chalets by the falls.

Ordinarily Katie would have taken the shortcut back to the mansion, past the graveyard. Today she decided to stick to the road, where she'd be able to see anyone approaching. Her caution was rooted in the fact that yesterday, she'd overheard a discussion between Freddie and Madge the cook.

"Some of them are calling it 'the servants disease' now," he'd said.

Cook had shaken his head. "Anything for a scapegoat. Why us, though? I'd have thought the old witch up the mountain would be the first one they'd go for."

"There's a rumour going round that we've been fucking the livestock."

There had been a solid *thunk* as Cook dropped a heavy ladle into a pot. "Sorry, come again?"

"I heard it from Lady Mark's butler. The idea is that one of us did it with an infected goat, and that was how it spread from animals to humans so quickly."

They'd both laughed at that—a brittle, nervous laughter.

As Katie strode home past the poisoned fields, she saw that many of the barley stalks had begun to sprout small pink buds, the shade reminiscent of the blossom that had grown from the deer's corpse.

Chapter Fourteen

Hermana, troubled by bad dreams, slept until dawn and was woken by a noise outside her window. Creeping out of the house with a heavy pot in hand in case Gregor and his mates had come back, she saw the goblin woman standing alone in the morning mist.

She was wearing butterflies. Dozens of them, red and black and very much alive, perched on her bare torso as though she were a flower. They added a shade of modesty, although her loincloth was even skimpier than last time—barely larger than a handkerchief, and leaving little to the imagination.

"Where've you been?" Hermana demanded. "What were you thinking, running off like that?"

The woman beckoned to her and started to walk towards the trees.

"Wait, wait. I need to get Ruth."

Soon, both of them were following the woman up the slope, drawing their sleeves across their noses to block out the smell. The butterflies trailed behind her like a living cape, and Hermana swatted at them. Ruth kept her eyes on the ground, fascinated by the flowers that sprang up in her footsteps.

The mushroom patch was worse than ever. Everything around them save for the corpse itself was soft and sticky and festering. And worse— the trees had begun to change. Many of those branches that hadn't fallen off now looked very much like skinny, grasping arms. At the base of their trunks, the wood had warped into shapes that bore a striking resemblance to toes. And on one old beech, there was a head. It grew straight out of the trunk, a rounded protrusion with three hollow cavities that a careless glance could easily mistake for eyes and a mouth. Everywhere Hermana looked, she saw wooden body parts.

The goblin woman pointed to the corpse's face, then to her own. She held out both hands, made them into a cup shape, and then slowly drew them against her face. It took a few repetitions for Hermana to work out that she was miming a kiss.

"He's your man?" she prompted. "Your husband?"

"How do we get rid of him?" said Ruth, red-eyed and ratty. Hermana suspected she had also had bad dreams. "We're out of ideas."

Hermana pantomimed their attempted burial and their pyre—though whether the woman interpreted the vague 'whooshing' motions she made as flames was anyone's guess.

The woman's hand went to the sheathed knife at her side that Hermana hadn't noticed before—her attention had been on the butterflies. She drew it, and they both took an instinctive step backwards before she placed it at Ruth's feet. She then performed a complicated pantomime of her own, which they watched in silence.

"Is she..." Hermana licked her lips. "Is she trying to tell us that..."

Ruth picked up the knife and tested its heft. "I think so. She wants us to cut his heart out."

She tilted her head to one side as the woman repeated the last part of her miming. "And eat it."

✳✳✳

"So, you or me?" Hermana asked as they shared the last of the peaches for breakfast. She'd already been back home and given four to Maggie. To her surprise, her grandmother had been doing some foraging of her own and had supplied her with a handful of clean berries. She'd also given her two eggs and a cupful of milk; though their vegetable garden lay fallow, their goats and chickens were still healthy.

"What?" said Ruth, gazing into the trees. The goblin woman had run off again as soon as she'd conveyed her message, and they'd both wondered where she went, and if she spoke to anyone else—and, if not, why she had chosen to speak to them.

"Who's going to eat it? Should we draw straws?"

"I thought we'd split it. I mean, we haven't got to eat it raw, right? We can use the knife, cut it up like mince, make enough stew to fill two bowls, and gulp it right down."

84

Hermana made a face. "Sounds awful."

"Well, we don't have much of choice, do we?"

"Ruthie, I've had a thought. She says the only way to get rid of the body is to eat the heart. Fair enough. It's magic; who knows how it works? But here's the question: why can't she eat it herself? She's his bit of stuff. So why does she want two complete strangers to eat it?"

That gave Ruth pause. She picked up the knife, fingered it, and said slowly, "They only reason I can think of is that it's dangerous."

Hermana nodded. "Right. Ruth, what if the heart's poisonous? The yellow stuff poisons everything, and it comes from him. Why if eating that heart polishes us off?"

Chapter Fifteen

The village had two graveyards.

The first was in a field behind the orchards, surrounded by a brick wall. Travellers coming upon it were often confused by the small pyramid of stones that sat at its entrance. These, in fact, were the remains of a shrine built by the valley's original owners centuries ago. In more recent years, the villagers had repurposed them into a memorial commemorating those who had died in the long battle to take the valley away from its original owners. The graveyard itself was neat and tidy, though somewhat rundown, with daisies and dandelions growing in the corners.

The second graveyard was well maintained, every headstone polished, every weed torn up. The headstones had been designed in the capital and transported to the valley at monumental expense. Every so often, the owners of the chalets by the waterfall would visit their deceased relatives in the second graveyard, bringing an entourage of children, servants, children's servants, servants' children, friends, and servants of friends. On those occasions, the graveyard took on the atmosphere of a springtime carnival, and many of the villagers would frown and mutter to themselves.

"Lord above, I hate dead people," said Gregor.

Beside him, Joan was busy entertaining theories as to why the second graveyard had been struck first. *Probably because it's closer to the river.*

"Waste of space. Waste of good land. Feed me to the pigs when I die, that's all I ask. None of this ceremonial nonsense. Would you look at that big stone angel—how much did that cost, do you think?"

"I've no idea," said Joan, opening the cemetery gates with the key that she'd had to apply to the mayor to obtain. "Right, let's brace ourselves."

The reason she was here instead of attending to any of the other hundred crises that awaited her attention was because several people had complained of strange noises coming from within the fancy folk's cemetery. Ordinarily, Joan would have assumed that one of the young noblemen, possibly Daniel, had brought his latest paramour there for a discreet bit of fooling around. She disapproved of that sort of thing—although her faith in God had wavered in recent years, she still regarded places where people were buried as sacred—but there wasn't much she could do about it. Her authority was limited where fancy folk were concerned.

As these were not ordinary times, and most of the young noblemen were holed up in their bedrooms for fear of getting sick, she had decided to look into the matter. She'd hoped that the venture would allow her a short respite from Gregor's attempts to be helpful; alas, he'd caught her on her way out.

Joan had a nasty suspicion that he wanted to court her. Oh, she didn't think he found her attractive—women like pretty Katie Bellows were more to his taste. But there were advantages to being married to a sheriff, and she knew that Gregor was far more sly than most people gave him credit for.

The gate swung open with a hideous creak, and Joan peered in. She'd expected the yellow muck coating the ground, and the withered grass. She wasn't surprised by the dead pigeons and moles scattered here and there, nor by the smell. What did surprise her were the graves themselves. Many of the headstones were cracked or toppled onto their sides, and Joan could see the edges of more than one coffin poking up from the rubble.

Gregor rubbed his chin, examining the nearest yellow patch as though it were a clue in a murder mystery. "Mmm. Yes, definitely the same stuff. I'd stake my life on it."

"Thank you, Mister Markbridge. In this time of confusion, your clear-headed deductions are invaluable to me." *You utter ponce.*

"Thanks, Sheriff, I... Bloody hell, Joan, look at those!"

Gregor pointed to the far end of the graveyard. Joan squeezed her eyes shut and then made herself open them again.

Five unfortunate souls, little more than bones kept together by the grace of their underclothes and strips of skin, hung in mid-air like scarecrows. They were being held up by a thick, eldritch vine that looked as though it might once have been ivy. Their heads lolled back, the plant growing into their skulls via their empty eye sockets and lacing between their ribs.

"That is quite something, that is," said Gregor, evidently fascinated.

Joan said nothing. She was sending thanks to God that all her relatives were either safely interred in the other graveyard or, in the case of her grandfather, in a small patch of grass on the edge of the woods that was reserved for the graves of servants and foreigners.

Gregor clasped his hands behind his back with an investigative air. "What I can't work out is how the headstones got knocked over. That vine's not strong enough, surely."

The answer to his query chose that moment to emerge from the ground, with a rumble and a sound of many legs scuttling.

It stopped and stared at them. It went, "Wuuaargh."

One of the reasons Joan was regarded as a decent sheriff by her community—despite her lax treatment of criminals—was that she was good at keeping her head. As Gregor gaped and stammered, she controlled her panic by listing its features in her head. Twenty feet long, the bulk of its body like that of a centipede. Thirty legs or thereabouts, all of unequal sizes, some of which ended in hoofs, and some in human feet. Its enormous mouth had no lower jaw, only a thick, lolling tongue that was so long it dragged on the ground, leaving a trail of yellow spots behind. She couldn't tell how it held itself together. Its spine was external and comprised of at least five other spines, none of which looked strong enough to support its grotesque body.

It stared at them for five seconds—Joan would remember each one for the rest of her life—and then it went, "Wuuargh," again. Watching it skitter back would have been fascinating, had there been several thick bars between Joan and it, for each leg moved differently, some at a different pace, some in a different direction, one not moving at all, but twitching feebly as though to convey willingness. All in all, it didn't look as though it should have been able to move at all, never mind so fast.

89

It retreated until it reached one of the defiled graves, and then, twisting its body into a figure eight, scuttled into it. In a flurry of earth and bits of dead people, it was gone.

"Look at it go!" cried Gregor in an exultant tone. "What about that, eh? What about *that*?"

Later, as they returned to the village, his excitement seemed to have worn off.

"This can't go on," he said, shaking his head. "Dirty water and bad smells and giant wriggling things. It's out of hand, Joan. I know you've been doing your best, but anyone can tell it's out of hand. Where'll it end? Someone needs to step up."

Joan wasn't listening. She had spotted Katie walking down the road with her basket and her clean white apron, and was trying to catch her eye to smile at her. If she'd been paying attention to Gregor's tone, and the emphasis he placed on 'someone', it would have occurred to her to worry.

Chapter Sixteen

"Ladies!"

After spending an hour arguing with Ruth over what to do about the heart, her stomach growing queasier and queasier at the prospect, the last thing in the world Hermana wanted was to see Daniel's handsome grin.

He had a new hat. It made him look like a dashing highwayman, and it only worsened her mood. Why were all the best things in the world reserved for people with no spots, people with all their teeth, people whose vowels were rounded when they said, "I've been looking for you *everywhere*, my doves. What are you up to?"

"Nothing," Ruth said as he dismounted.

"Ruth, Ruth. You really are a terrible liar. Mind you, I suppose I've had more practice. You never had to keep a straight face while telling your schoolmaster a porky."

Sod you. She's a brilliant liar, rich boy.

Despite Hermana's instinctive irritation, she noticed that Daniel looked a touch under the weather. His eyes were bloodshot, and his complexion was greyer than usual. The thought occurred to her that he might have caught the forest's sickness, and when Ruth stepped towards him and put a hand on his brow, she had to fight the urge to pull her back.

"You all right, Daniel?" Ruth asked.

"Oh, yes. Fine. Fine."

She sniffed. "You smell like you've been drinking. Is..."

"Who punched you?" said Hermana, noticing the faint purpling around his left eye.

"Oh, it wasn't a punch. It..." He stopped, swallowed. "More of a clout, really. I don't think he meant to. He seemed to be aiming for my

91

ear. He was a touch drunk."

"Who?"

"My father. To be honest with you, he's been out of sorts of late. All the...strangeness has been unnerving him. He's talked about moving back to the capital. Anyway, what set him off this morning were his hounds. They've been sick for a week; we thought they were finally getting better, then they both died at dawn, one right after the other. Father loved them, and he...he's taken it rather badly. I came upon him clutching the bodies, and I made the mistake of suggesting that in doing so he might run the risk of infection."

"And he did that to you?" said Ruth, her voice rich with sympathy. Hermana didn't fully understand why; from the looks of things, it hadn't been much of a punch. Back when Ruth's uncle had been alive, she'd seen Ned sporting far worse injuries. "That's awful, Daniel. Listen, why don't you come home with us? We can have some tea, and there's...actually, there's something I wanted to talk to you about."

Hermana looked at Ruth sharply. *God, she's going to tell him. Why? How can he help us? The only things he's good for are hunting, horse riding, and praying in dead languages.*

Daniel touched Ruth's cheek. "That's very kind of you, Ruth. But what I'd rather do instead is take you back to the chalet with me. You did promise you'd come—remember? I could introduce you to him. He'd like you, I'm sure of it. He's been asking me why I spend so much time in the woods. Meeting you might...might alleviate some of his concerns. How about it, eh, Ruth?"

"Daniel, if your dad's pissed and grieving, do you think showing up with me on your arm's going to make it better? He'll hit the roof. No nobleman's going to be happy that his only boy's been gallivanting about with a girl like me."

"He's different, Ruth. He's a kind man, an honourable man."

"A kind man who beats up his kid over a dead dog," Hermana said archly. "She's right, Daniel. He might chase you out of the house. Lord knows what he might do to her."

Daniel looked from her to Ruth. "I...I can protect you Ruth."

Straightening up, Ruth said, "I don't want you to protect me. And I don't want to meet your father. Not today, anyway. I've work to do, and lots of it. You can come home with me if you don't want to go back your dad's chalet alone. We'll hide you for as long as you want. But I'm not coming with you."

Daniel rubbed his eyes, and then the bridge of his nose. He seemed older suddenly. In a new voice, a brittle voice, he said, "All right. Cards on the table. You're eighteen, and I'm twenty-two; we should be able to discuss this like adults. The fact of the matter is that it's been a few years now, Ruth. You do realise that's more time—more effort—than I have put into literally every other girl I've ever met? My God, that's more time and effort than I've put into *anything*. I think I've done my bit, is the point. Made the effort. Done the gentlemanly thing. I know you're odd, but I've never held it against you."

He paused, in a manner suggesting that the appropriate response at this point would be a gracious acknowledgement and a small gesture of thanks. When neither was forthcoming, he continued. "And, fine, let's put it out there. I am, beyond all reasonable doubt, the only chance at a decent life you are ever likely to have. I'm not trying to be rude. It's just the truth. You know it's the truth. What are your alternatives, realistically speaking? Do you think you'll marry a servant from the village and sit around raising a dozen of his children? Or stay on this mountain all your life and marry a fox? There's no *future* for you here, Ruth. No opportunities. Be sensible. You're a bright girl. In fact, I think you're the brightest girl I know. And you're going to waste."

"Right, that's enough," said Hermana, because Ruth was looking more and more hurt.

"No, I'm not done!" he said, almost shouting. "Ruth, I can take you away from this place. I can give you the sort of life you should have. And I might well be your only hope. You've no education. Your face is lovely, but it won't last forever. Your complexion... *I* think you're stunning, I truly do, but the fact is that it'll close a lot of doors, Ruth. I could wedge those doors open. If you'd only *let* me."

"You don't talk to her like that!" Hermana snarled.

He glared at her. "Can you call her off, Ruth? I'm trying to get my point across, and she's not helping. I know she's never liked me, and I don't care for her much, either."

Hermana stuck a finger in his face. "You listen to me..."

"No, I don't think I will, and please clean your fingernails. You bite them so often one shudders to think of all the bacteria you must be transferring to your wide and scowling mouth. I am having a conversation with Ruth, not with you. May I say that, of all the factors holding your friend back from achieving her full potential, *you* are chief among them?"

Hermana's arm dropped to her side, and a thick, hot lump formed in the back of her throat.

"You encourage her to run about like a savage," Daniel continued, folding his arms across his chest. "You distract her keen intellect with your infantile infatuation with these woods. She's prettier than you, and far more intelligent, so you do your best to bring her down to your level. I don't think you're her friend at all. You're a leech, a parasite, trying to hide a truly unique girl away from the world to satisfy your jealousy. It's all rather sad, in my opinion. Don't you understand that she could have achieved something by now? She could be a nobleman's wife. She could have a coterie of friends to talk to and shop with. She could have had so *many* things, and all she has is *you*."

A second later he howled as Ruth's bony knee connected with his groin.

"You say one more word, Daniel, and I'll send you back to your dad with your bits off," she said, and he slapped her.

Later, Hermana would be willing to admit that there had been mitigating circumstances. He was upset. He was drunk. Instinct and anger had probably driven his hand more than a desire to hurt.

At that moment, none of that mattered. All she felt was rage. A lifetime of carrying water from the river to her house had built up the muscles in her arms, and when she charged, she sent them both sprawling. The horse whinnied as she punched its master in the face as hard as she could, then again, and again, and on the fourth punch she missed. He drove an elbow into her gut, winding her, and shoved her off. Then they were on each other like dogs fighting over a bone.

She never really had a chance. While she was stronger than he was, it had been years since she'd gotten into a proper fight with anyone, and Daniel had had training. As she grabbed hold of his hair, he caught her by the arm, twisting it until she yelled, then kicked out her knees beneath her. As soon as she was on the ground, he stepped down hard on her wrist. Her eyes watered as she felt bones begin to shift, and the prospect of climbing up the mountain one-handed for the rest of her life prompted her to claw frantically at his leg.

Then she heard Ruth's voice: "Get off her! Please, Daniel, I'll do whatever you want!"

She's begging. She's begging, because of me.

Hermana had never despised herself more.

Daniel lifted up his boot. She gasped and curled up, clutching it between her thighs to dull the pain. Ruth dropped to her side, touching her hair, her skin.

"She's fine," he mumbled, his face flushed and his lip split open. "I didn't hurt her that much. She's putting it on. Ruth, she's..."

He stopped short. Ruth had taken the goblin's knife out of its sheath and was pointing it at him.

"*Go away,*" she hissed.

He started back as though she'd struck him. Then his eyes hardened.

"I'm not angry," he said. "I am disappointed. They all warned me about you two, but I decided to give you a chance. I really did think... Well, it doesn't matter. Good day."

He mounted his horse and rode away at speed.

Hermana grabbed Ruth's leg, tripping her up as she started to go after him. "For God's sake, Ruth, don't give him an excuse."

"You're one to talk!" snarled Ruth, murder in her eyes. "Get off; I'm going to box his ears in!"

Hermana caught her by the scruff. "It won't do any good. It'll only make an enemy of him. No one can protect us from the likes of him, you understand? Not the law, not my gran, not anyone. He's always going to be more powerful than the two of us, no matter what. Everything you do to him now is something he'll make you apologise for later. Don't make it worse, Ruthie. Don't."

95

"You knew what he was like. Shit, I should have—"

"No, I didn't know. I thought he was richer and smarter than me, and I thought he'd take you away with him. That's why I didn't like him. I was jealous."

For a moment, the only sound was their panting. Then Ruth slammed her fist into the dirt.

Hermana's head throbbed like mad. As they walked back, Ruth kept one arm around her waist in case she fainted. Every last inch of her hurt. Her stomach, shoulders, legs, even her tits were a mass of bruises.

The worst part was that she was happy. A guilty sort of happiness. She was self-aware enough to realise how much she had hoped and prayed that Daniel would turn out to be wicked. Then she'd have a reason to hate him, a reason to tell Ruth that she should stay away from him. Maybe, in wishing so hard, she had *made* him bad.

What fuelled her guilt, though, was not so much anything she might have done to Daniel. Nor was it the bruises or the scrapes. She'd had worse; she'd spent her adolescence falling from the tops of trees and running from the villager's dogs.

No, her guilt had to do with the grey misery haunting Ruth's eyes, and the memory of her voice as she'd begged.

Chapter Seventeen

Katie was worried about the sheriff.

She'd long nurtured a fondness for handsome Joan Bailey, with her warm smiles and low, throaty voice. Ever since Katie had heard the story of how Joan had flogged the mountain girls to within an inch of their lives, she'd like her even more. Whenever Joan passed by the mansion she'd greet her and offer her tea, and Joan would tip her sheriff's hat and express deepest regret that she was too busy to accept the offer. Both of them knew that Mistress would never have permitted a common keeper of the law onto her property, and both recognised the exchange as a show of mutual understanding that the world was not what they wanted it to be.

Recently, Joan hadn't come by the mansion at all. She was too busy trying to keep the village under control. In addition to helping the mayor and the priest put plans into motion for when the food ran out, she had recruited two dozen men and women to help aid the sickly. It wasn't easy, she had imparted to Katie on her last visit. Many were too afraid to go near the infected.

Katie herself was terrified that Joan would fall ill. She'd even thought about going to see Maggie Dim and asking her for some spell or potion that would keep the sheriff safe. But everyone was saying that the village's witch had abandoned them to their fate. Certainly, she hadn't come down from her home in the mountain since the river had turned putrid. There were even rumours going round that she may, in some way, be responsible.

Katie didn't believe a word of it, and she worried for poor old Missus Dim as she worried for Joan, and Charlie, and herself. As the village's situation worsened and the portions she and the other servants received at mealtimes grew smaller and smaller, she would lie awake at night and wish that she were stronger, richer, and cleverer. That she were God and could fix the world with a wave of her hand.

"Something's up," said Freddie one afternoon not long after Joan had encountered the horror at the cemetery. "Mistress wants everyone upstairs now."

They all assembled and were told that the mayor had called for every able-bodied man and woman in the village to converge on the Danters' farm forthwith, with water, spades, and sacks.

"Why? What's happening?" Freddie said to Mistress.

"I hardly think it's your place to ask questions, Frederick," Mistress replied, fingering her little book.

The Danters' farm was the oldest in the valley and belonged to its two oldest people. Mrs and Mister Danters had a combined age of two hundred and one, and they owned more cats than all the surrounding farms combined. Apart from its age, theirs was unremarkable; smaller than most, less productive than most, employing fewer men than most. Its most notable features were Mister Danters's pumpkins, which had won first prize at the provincial fair three times in the last ten years.

By the time Katie and the others got there, it was late evening. The sun was setting, and torches had been lit.

"What's that for?" asked Freddie, pointing to a makeshift barricade of sacks and barrels that had been set up at the edge of the Danters' wheat field.

One of the Danters' strapping young nephews ran up to them and accepted Katie's water gratefully, sweat pouring down his face.

"They won't stop coming," he said to them when he had caught his breath. "One of them tried to run up Duffy's leg! Should have heard him yell!"

Someone called his name, and he ran off. Katie and Freddie exchanged looks and, putting aside their load, crawled up the side of the barricade and looked down into the fields beyond.

"Oh my God," said Freddie, his face shining in the firelight.

At a glance, it looked as though the rich, dark soil in which the Danters grew their prize-winning pumpkins had come to life. A second glance revealed that it was not the ground which was wriggling, but a seething horde of vermin; field mice, squirrels, moles and rats. Here and there, Katie spotted birds, a lark or a shrike, hopping amongst the squeaking, squealing masses.

It took a third glance to see that the swarming mice and squirrels had lost most of their fur, and that ugly yellow tumours were sprouting from their backs. Pus oozed from their ears, and many of them were without claws, teeth, or eyes. The birds didn't take flight because their wings no longer had enough feathers to support them. A mockingbird, which had been able to flutter his way halfway up one of the stalks, pecked in vain at an ear of wheat; his beak had fallen off.

"There's so many," whispered Freddie, and indeed, the ground was black with them. The crops bent sideways, weighted down by dozens of tiny, tortured bodies.

Twenty or so people were moving through the field with big boots on and open sacks. They used rakes and pitchforks to shepherd the animals into them, and when the sacks were full they took them to a pyre burning at the edge of the field.

"More bags! More bags needed here!" someone yelled.

"All ours are full!" someone shouted back.

"Where's the water?"

"Where's the sheriff?"

"Oh, God! One of them bit me!"

Katie looked around for Joan and found her standing by the pyre. She had taken off her hat and her jacket, and stood atop a barrel directing the hunters.

"We need more men," she was shouting. "Where's Gregor? You, be careful with that torch."

Katie waved, and even through the smoke, she could see Joan's expression brighten.

"Thank you, Miss Bellows," she said, when Katie had made her way over to her and given her water to drink.

"Where have they come from, Sheriff?" Katie asked.

"Hell would be my first guess," she said and then blushed. "I apologise. That was coarse."

"It's fine," said Katie, although ordinarily she looked upon cursing as a sign of low character. "Are you...are you all right?"

Joan took another mouthful of water. "I'm hanging in there. I'm a touch on edge—my boy Sam woke up with yellow spots this morning. I'd hoped to be home with him by now. He's only got the cat for company."

Katie had met Sam Bailey once or twice and had liked him. He'd have made a good playmate for Charlie, if Mistress hadn't strongly discouraged her servants from socialising outside the mansion.

"I could go and read to him," she volunteered. "If you've got no use for me here, I mean. Mistress said we were to stay and help until things were sorted out."

The sheriff gave her a hopeful smile. "That's generous of you. Er— I must warn you, my house might come as a bit of a shock. I keep it clean, and we've no mice, but it's... Well, it's small and a bit dilapidated. Nothing like the mansion."

"I'm sure it's lovely," said Katie. *What fine eyes she has. Why do people say she looks like a man? Does no one ever really look at her? I suppose not. If they did, she'd be married by now.*

"Katie-girl!"

"Oh, balls," muttered Joan, her whole body wincing. "Apologies again, miss."

Gregor, in the process of throwing another bag of vermin onto the pyre, waved at them.

"Hello, Mister Markbridge," Katie said. She didn't care for Gregor, nor his flirtations, and feared that to reject him outright would only encourage him. So she had an array of bland smiles to shield herself with whenever they met.

"I think Mister Markbridge has been drinking," Joan said out the corner of her mouth. "It's my own fault. I should have been keeping a closer eye on him. Like all of us, he's been taking strain these past few days."

Gregor staggered over to them, swaying, and gave Katie an exaggerated bow. "Her ladyship arrives! How are you, Kates, eh?"

"I'm well, Mister Markbridge. Thank you. The sheriff was telling me all about the good work you've been doing."

"Oh, yes. Lots of work. Lots of hard, nasty work. Not easy for men like me, you know. Slaving away, keeping the...the rats and the giant centipedes from your Mistress's door. Don't mind admitting that I'm in the mood for a spot of gratitude. How about it? After we finished tidying up this mess, how about you and me go the tavern... have a nice little drink?"

"What a lovely thought. I'm afraid I've already promised Sheriff Bailey that I—"

Gregor blew a raspberry. "To the devil with Bailey. Dreadful woman. Absolute bitch, between you and me."

Has he not noticed her? Does he not care that she can hear him?

"Be that as it may, I'm sure Miss Bellows does not care for that sort of language," growled Joan, and Gregor craned his head back to stare at her, blinking.

"Hell, Bailey, where'd you come from?" he slurred. "Standing there all quiet like a...like a fish. No noise. I...er. I thought you might be elsewhere."

He hiccoughed and turned his attention back to Katie. "Listen, Kat... Kates, what do you make of all this? Never mind—I'll tell you what I think. I think it's the cow. You know. *Her.* The old witch up the mountain, with her pig and her tart of a granddaughter. They've been up to mischief. Mark my words, they're sitting up there laughing at us."

Thankfully, at that moment a two-headed mole ran over his foot, and he set about trying to step on it.

"I should be getting on," Katie said to Joan, before he could continue his diatribe. "I'll take care of your Sam; don't worry."

"Thank you, Miss Bellows."

"Goodnight, Sheriff. And good luck."

She left Joan with Gregor draped against her side. He was starting to sing, his voice ringing out over the crackle and roar of the blaze.

The next morning, the air was thick with ash, and what remained of the Danters' harvest was a grey gash on the landscape. A pit was dug beside the smouldering earth, into which hundreds of small, smoking bodies were swept.

Chapter Eighteen

Maggie sat in her favourite chair, her pig in her lap, staring at nothing.

From outside the house, Hermana kept an eye on her through the window. Ever since Ned's death, her grandmother had remained sunk in gloom. Hermana had never known her to be so inactive.

"She blames herself for what happened to Ned," said Ruth. "You and I know she did the best she could, but she'll never accept that. She's a healer. And remember that she was with him at the last. She saw..."

She paused, swallowed, and continued, "She saw the worst of it. It's hardly surprising she's not herself. Give her time."

They sat not ten yards from Hermana's front door, in a patch of lavender; for some reason, it seemed less susceptible to the poison than other flowers. It also helped to drown out the smell.

Returning to the topic at hand, Hermana said, "The more I think about it, the more I'm certain that that heart's poisonous. Why else would she choose us to eat it? She knows there's not many people who'd miss us, that's why. Well, sod that. I don't want to die. I mean, fine, no one wants to die, but I've got things I want to do first."

Ruth had been staring reflectively up at the canopy. Now she shrugged and said, "I suppose we should get Daniel to eat it, then."

Hermana lifted her head from her knees and stared at her with wide eyes.

"There's not many people who'd miss him, either," Ruth continued. "His mother's dead, and he's got no kids. His friends are back in the capital. His dad would be upset, but we could get him a new dog to make up for it. And I can't see the villagers giving a shit. All he does is hunt and drink and muck about with his horses. He's not any use to anyone."

"That...that's all true, I s'pose..."

"Why're you looking at me like that?"

103

"Um. It's a bit cold-blooded, isn't it?"

Ruth's jaw was set, and her eyes had that hard, polished look to them that said that she'd already made her decision. "Look, I don't want to die, and you don't want to die, and if someone *has* to die, it may as well be someone no one would miss much. Daniel's not got any responsibilities, no family who'll starve if he's gone. It makes sense."

Hermana chewed the inside of her cheek. "It does. Right. Fine. So how do we get him to do it?"

They spent the next two hours formulating plans and discarding them. Ruth came up with the most creative—they could sneak into the kitchen of his father's chalet in disguise, pretend to be new cooks sent from the capital, and then try to pass the heart off as an exotic and fashionable new food fad. Hermana came up with the most practical—hit him on the head with a rock, tie him to a tree and force him to eat at knifepoint. Ruth's plan was dismissed on the grounds of limited resources—they didn't have wigs, nor makeup, nor did either of them know anything about cooking for fancy people. Hermana's plan was dismissed because neither was certain they'd have the nerve when it came to it.

"I mean, it sounds all right in theory," said Ruth. "But then we've got him there in front of us, and he's crying and begging for his life, we might start to feel sorry for the bugger."

"I wouldn't feel sorry for him," Hermana said but eventually conceded that while she had no problem with being complicit in the removal of Daniel from this plain of existence, the raw reality of force-feeding someone poison might be more than she could take.

"Seems to me that the easiest way to do it is to make him *want* to eat it," said Ruth.

"How do you make someone want to eat a goblin's heart?"

Ruth mulled this over for a while, before saying, "You make him think he'll get something out of it. Something he really wants. Something he wants more than he *doesn't* want to eat a heart."

They looked at one another.

"Ruthie, you're not actually suggesting you go up to him and say, 'Hello, tell you what—eat this heart, and I'll drop my knickers'."

"It's a thought."

"It's stupid," said Hermana. The very idea made her gut clench. "It might have worked before you knocked his balls in. But not now. He's a proud man. Even if he's still keen on you, he won't forgive you for that."

"We need to sweeten the deal, then. We'll tell him that if he eats the heart, I'll have ten of his children, and he'll live forever. 'Cause it's a *magic* heart, see."

"You think he'll buy that? Fancy folk don't believe in magic so easily as normal folk do."

Ruth gestured to the nearest tree, whose bark had taken on the look and the texture of rotting flesh. "Hermie, considering what's been going on for the last few weeks, I don't think it'll be that much of a chore to convince him. We can show him the corpse. We can show him its ears."

"And what if he asks how we know that the only way to get rid of it is to eat its heart?"

"Easy. We'll say that there's an old local legend about it. He's not from around these parts; he won't know any better. The legend says that if a handsome young man of noble birth finds a dead goblin and eats its heart, it means he's the chosen one and he'll live forever. Or whatever. He'll swallow that."

"Yeah...he just might."

They continued to debate the logistics as the sun descended. It took, altogether, almost an hour for Hermana to have a crisis of conscience.

"Um," Hermana said, embarrassed at the sudden swell of squeamishness, "shouldn't we be a bit more bothered by this? We are talking about really, literally killing a human being. I never thought I'd do that. Did you? It's just... It's weird, isn't it?"

"Nah. Everyone thinks about killing someone, now and then. They never talk about it, that's all."

"You think so?"

"I was going to kill Uncle, once," Ruth said matter-of-factly. "He kicked Ned in the gut and made him puke blood. I thought he'd die. I thought, 'Right, if Ned goes, so do you'. I made a proper plan and everything. Was going to go to the patch and get a few of the dangerous mushrooms, grind them up and put them in his stew, then bury him under the house where no one would find him. Then Ned and me would come and live with you and Maggie. But Ned got better, and I knew that he wouldn't approve. So I didn't go through with it."

"You never told me," Hermana accused. "I'd have helped, if you'd said. Hell, I'd have done it myself."

Ruth smiled and punched her arm. "I know that, stupid. I didn't think you wouldn't help. I just didn't want to get you involved. You were a cute kid, you know? Seemed wrong to mess that up."

Daniel's slap had left a faint mark on her skin, Hermana noticed.

"You've got one of your odds looks on," Ruth noted, tilting her head. "What're you thinking?"

"That he was right. You could be a nobleman's wife by now. You could live in a big city. Go to a fancy school. Ride around the world on a big horse. Or travel across the sea. You could do anything, Ruthie."

"You think so? Even with my wonky teeth?"

"Yeah."

"And my dirty fingernails?"

"Yeah."

Ruth smirked, tossing her hair back. "Of course I could."

"So...so why're you still here, then?"

Hermana hadn't noticed it happening, but at some point their faces had drifted closer together.

Instead of answering her, Ruth whispered, "What you said earlier... Were you telling the truth? Were you always such a shit to Daniel because you were jealous?"

Hermana nodded, and Ruth threw back her head and cackled. "Oh Lord almighty. That's pathetic, Hermie. That is... Oh, bloody hell. You're an idiot. You're *such* an idiot. Keep your face still."

Ruth's thin, powerful fingers bit into her jaw, making her lips seem even softer by comparison.

Before Hermana could fully work out what was happening, it was over. Ruth hopped to her feet and said, "I'm going to go get ready. We'll meet back here and head up to the chalet in one hour."

In the event, persuading a grown man that cutting open a corpse and devouring its heart was in his own best interest was surprisingly easy.

On their way up to the chalet, it started to drizzle. Ruth leaned back as she walked so the rain would wet her shirt and make it cling to her breasts. She also rubbed at her eyes to make them red, as though she'd been crying.

"The look we're going for is repentant," she said. "Repentant and dishy. Plait my hair."

"You look more dishy with it loose."

"Yeah, but he'll like to see think that I've made an effort for him. That's important too."

When they got there, Daniel was standing by the high brick wall surrounding the chalet, the rain kept off his shoulders by a heavy coat. He was overseeing a group of men and women who were on their hands and knees sprinkling something onto the ground—or rather, onto the lumps and pools of yellow muck staining the ground. Upon examining one of the open canvas bags beside them, Hermana discovered that what they were sprinkling was salt.

"What's that supposed to do?" she asked, before remembering that Ruth had told her to keep her mouth shut.

Daniel stiffened when he saw them, and for a moment, Hermana thought he might yell for someone to escort them off the premises. Then his eyes flicked to Ruth, and to Ruth's chest. Not smiling, but politely enough, he said, "Father's advice. He's consulted a witch from the capital. She says that the disease is caused by evil spirits. Salt will dispel them."

"A real witch?" said Ruth.

"Highly recommended, or so Father says. She has a certificate."

"Right."

"Can I help you, Ruth?"

The chilly disdain in his voice was enough to make Hermana want to plant another fist in his eye.

"We need to talk, Daniel," Ruth said. "Not here. Somewhere we can be alone. I'm sorry we had a fight and for everything I said. I know you don't think well of me at the moment. This is really, really important, though. I'd not have come if it wasn't. We need your help, Daniel."

The way they'd rehearsed it, this was where Hermana was supposed to say that she was sorry too. She couldn't. The words curled up in the back of her throat and wouldn't be brought forward. She dropped her eyes and let her shoulders slump, hoping that she looked cowed and penitent.

He made them wait while he thought about it. "I suppose you'd better come inside, then. We'll talk in the study."

They followed in his footsteps as he lead them up the garden path and in through the front door, earning a sideways glance from a footman. As they progressed down a well-lit corridor, Hermana stared in wonder at the patterned wallpaper, the rows and rows of lamps shaped like tulips, the soft, deep red carpet. After walking roughly the distance from Hermana's house to Ruth's, Daniel took them into a room with two large sofas and two dozen heads mounted on the walls.

Pouring himself a drink, Daniel said, "Sherry for either of you? All I have at the moment, I'm afraid. Father's physician's forbidden me from alcohol for the duration of my recovery. One of my chums managed to sneak this into the house for me."

"What're you recovering from?" Hermana asked.

He arched an eyebrow at her. "You."

Bristling, she said, "You knocked me about well enough, I didn't need a physician."

"Hermie, shut up," said Ruth. "Daniel, I know how to stop it."

"'It'?"

"The poison. The yellow stuff."

"Ah. Do you? I confess to some degree of scepticism. My father's brainiest horticulturalists have been puzzling over that one for weeks."

"I spoke to Hermana's grandmother. Maggie Dim."

That was their trump card. Like everyone else who lived in or around the valley, Daniel had heard of Maggie Dim. He sat up a little bit straighter. "How is the good woman?"

"She's worried," said Ruth, gravely. "Truth be told, she sent us to find you. She says... Daniel, she says that you're the only one who can save us."

That was the pivotal moment. Hermana watched his face. *Did you ever want to be a hero, eh, Danny? Yes, I think you did. You've no idea what she's talking about, but you're already imagining yourself our saviour, aren't you? Ruth's got your measure, rich boy.*

They told him about the corpse in the mushroom patch and their failed efforts to get rid of it. They left out various details, including the goblin woman and their fears of being poisoned. They brought Maggie into it, saying that she'd told them the valley was being cursed by the corpse's restless spirit, and that it would take a young man of noble blood and a pure heart to lay it to rest.

He lapped it up, every word. The sherry might have helped, as well as the fact that Ruth sat down beside him on the sofa, their legs brushing, and kept her voice low and conspiratorial so that he had to lean in close to hear her.

Hermana endured it. To pass the time, she examined the heads. A stag, a boar, a female black bear—whoever had stuffed them had managed to immortalise an expression of startled dismay, as though they had hoped to end their days mounted on the walls of better men.

"Why the heart? Why not the brain? Or the whole thing?" Daniel was asking.

Improvising, Ruth said, "Maggie said that the heart's the bit that his soul's tied to. When that's gone, his soul will be free, and the rest of him'll rot away normally."

Clever, Ruthie.

Daniel studied his empty glass. "And what if I said 'no'? If I relocated back to the capital with Father tomorrow—what would you do then?"

Ruth slid off the sofa and onto her knees. "Danny, if you don't stop it, no one will. Maggie said that the valley's only the beginning. When it's killed every tree in the forest, the yellow stuff's going to keep spreading out, east, west, north and south, and when it reaches the sea it'll kill all the fish and keep going. Don't you understand?"

She bit her lip and gave a gentle sob, burying her face in her hands. Hermana, who had heard what Ruth sounded like when she really was crying, almost cackled.

Daniel seemed to be about to drop down and embrace her, before catching himself. "I see. And tell me, Ruth..."

"Oh, don't make me beg," she whimpered. "Please, Daniel. We're all so frightened. Won't you help us?"

Don't overdo it. Hermana glanced towards the door, fearful that a butler or maid might wander in and spoil the mood.

Daniel took Ruth's hand in a gentlemanly fashion, and as he stood up so did she. "Ruth. Please. Enough. It pains me to see your pride so wounded. You must know I...I'm very fond of you. I always have been. I will do it, Ruth. I'll eat your heart and save your woods. I ask one thing in return."

"What, Danny?" said Ruth, blinking her wet eyes.

"A kiss. One sweet kiss from the girl I love. Nothing more."

Hermana closed her eyes. When she opened them, Daniel was blushing.

"Goodness, that was... Thank you, Ruth. I say, you are a spirited girl, aren't you? Right, let's get to it. I've a few things I need to take care of here first— Father's still in mourning for his hounds, so I'm running the place. Shall we meet in, say, four hours? Before sunset?"

As they left the chalet, Hermana vented her frustration on a muck-coated stone, kicking it like a ball down the slope.

"I didn't like it any more than you did," Ruth said, sounding tired.

"I know. God, he's a shit."

Before they reached the house, Hermana turned and seized her hands. "Ruthie, promise me you won't miss him. Or that if you do miss him, you won't miss him forever."

Ruth looked thoughtful, and Hermana had a sudden, vivid memory of the first time they'd met. It was one of the earliest memories she had.

She'd been eight years old, and her parents had been fighting. One of their last fights; two weeks later her father had left, never to return. Hermana couldn't remember what the fight had been about, though she did recall her father ripping out a handful of her mother's hair, and Maggie trying to keep her mother from clawing out his eyes in retaliation. She had a sneaking suspicion it had been about her; later on, Ruth had told her that she'd had a black eye when she'd found her. For the life of her, Hermana couldn't recollect how she'd received it.

Back then the riverbank had been one of her favourite hiding spots for those occasions when she never wanted to go back home. On that day, it had been raining hard. The water was higher and rougher than usual, and the bank was slippery with mud.

By the time two strong, skinny arms had wrapped around her waist and dragged her out, Hermana had been underwater for almost two minutes and was under the impression that she was already dead. She recalled the sensation of a tiny fist pounding on her ribcage, the sharp, painful light through the trees as she'd opened her eyes, and the taste of river water as she'd been rolled onto her side and puked it up.

"This is my river" had been the first thing the other girl had said, while Hermana had gazed up at her and wondered if she was from heaven. "What are you playing at, drowning in it? You want your smelly body to kill all my fish?"

Gazing at her now, Hermana thought, *I'm glad I got to grow up with you. Whatever happens next, I'm still glad.*

"I'll miss him," Ruth allowed. "I'll be upset for a while, most likely. He had his good parts. But the thing is, Hermie, I saw his face when he was stepping on your arm. He looked the way Uncle used to look when he was kicking Ned. I can't forgive him for that. Not ever. Probably makes me a horrible person, but I was never a *great* person to begin with. Right, let's go over the plan one more time..."

Chapter Nineteen

Another five people had died in the night. Three more had been declared missing, having gone into the woods to hunt for food two days ago. Many-eyed rats and greasy black maggots crawled through the streets, bringing with them a stink so strong it made grown men retch. All the fields and farmland surrounding the village were full of dead crops and giant, otherworldly flowers that attacked anyone who got too close.

Katie wasn't surprised to see the crowd gathered in the town square, listening to Gregor bellow about witches from atop an overturned beer barrel.

"It was always going to happen," Freddie said, watching with her. "Sooner or later, they'd find someone to blame. We should be grateful it's not us."

Katie knew that the people amongst whom she had been born and raised, into whose company her grandmother had been sold and whose faces she knew as well as she knew her own, were not complicated people. They were competent people. They had to be, to thrive in a valley where sheep and cattle outnumbered the populace by a ratio of three to one, where the winters were biting, and the nearest major city was countless miles eastwards. Incompetence was squeezed out of them like juice from fruit. But they weren't complicated. They believed in a simple, orderly world, where rules were rules, where some people were worth more than other people, and where any problem, no matter how complicated, could be solved with hot tea, prayer, or a noose.

"Most of them are laughing at him," said Katie, noting all those members of the crowd who were covering smiles with their hands or sharing giggles and whispers with their friends.

"Not all of them are laughing," Freddie said and did not need to say: *Not enough of them are laughing.*

As Katie watched, torches and pitchforks were distributed. About twenty of the onlookers took one or the other, most of them young men, Gregor's drinking mates.

"Someone should get the sheriff," she said, a quaver in her voice. The torches were held up with a cheer that told her the drink had been passed round. Those who'd come to laugh wandered away, so that later, if asked, they could say they hadn't known what Gregor was planning.

"Joan's busy in the fields," said Freddie. "The priest's in his study, trying to work out a way to pray things back to normal. The mayor's locked himself in his home. No one's going to stop them."

Katie looked towards the trees, their shadows growing long now that the sun was setting. "Then someone should run ahead to give a warning. There's...there's a shortcut..."

"It'd be dangerous," said Freddie. "I wouldn't go into those woods now, not even with an army to back me. Besides, she can take care of herself. She's a tough old bird. Let's go home, Katie."

Gregor's men began to sing boisterously as they made their way down the road that would take them into the woods, their boots sending up a cloud of dust.

Katie thought of the dinner table she was supposed to be laying, the bed sheets she was supposed to have turned down by now, the bath that she needed to pour, the fire that needed poking, and the sheet music that needed to be laid out for Mistress's after-dinner recital. She thought of the stinking fox pelt, and of the old, tired-looking woman who'd shaken her hand and told her she'd make a great and terrible God.

"Freddie, I need you to give Charlie his dinner for me. Tell him I'll be back soon. If you see Joan Bailey, tell her where I've gone. No, wait, don't tell her. She'd got enough to worry about. Just tell her that... No, don't tell her that either. I'll tell her myself."

"Be careful!" Freddie shouted after her as she started to run.

***

Hermana couldn't eat her dinner. Not that there was much of it; boiled roots and a few pigeon eggs her grandmother had miraculously procured. Every time she tried raising a mouthful to her lips, she had a vision of Daniel biting into the red meat of a still-beating heart.

Don't be stupid. It won't be beating. He's been dead for ages.

Perhaps that didn't matter. Perhaps goblin hearts never stopped beating. Perhaps if Daniel swallowed it and it didn't kill him, it would continue to beat in his stomach for the rest of his life.

Stop it.

"Are you all right, dear? You're awfully quiet," said her grandmother.

"I'm fine, Gran. Thinking, that's all."

How much longer now? She ran over the plan in her head. Daniel would come down from the chalet, and Ruth would lead him to the mushroom patch. Hermana would follow behind them, lurking in the shadows; if Daniel was having second thoughts, her presence would only put him off. She would arrive at the mushroom patch when he was already getting stuck in. If he got squeamish halfway through, the two of them would knock him over and make him finish, with Ruth's knife at his neck if necessary. Then, if he died, they'd bury the body as deep as they could. For that, Hermana would need her shovel, another reason for her lagging behind Daniel and Ruth. Wouldn't want him getting suspicious.

Watching Maggie eat her roots, the pig sleeping on her lap, Hermana thought, *Does he have a grandmother? He never said. Will she miss him?*

Hermana knew she wasn't a good person. Good people went to church and married nice boys and loved their parents—or mourned them, at least. Village girls were good people. Sheriff Bailey was a good person. Little Katie who brought charity and wore a bonnet was a good person. By anyone's standards, Hermana wasn't a good person. By the same token, she'd never thought of herself as a bad one. Like foxes and fish, she and Ruth and Maggie were exempt from the rules of village morality; that was what she'd always told herself.

But even in terms of village morality... She and Ruth had never done anything that bad, had they? Alright, throwing the fox at Katie had been mean-spirited. The apples they'd nicked from the orchard last summer—they hadn't needed those; they hadn't been starving. And,

115

fine, she'd once prayed that Daniel would fall off his horse, break a leg, and never come back to the valley for the rest of his life.

That was little stuff, though. The big stuff, the important stuff—she'd never had a problem with any of that. Maggie had instilled the basics of Not Being Very Bad into her at a young age: *Don't hit your kids; don't steal from your friends; don't touch anyone where they don't want to be touched; don't kick dogs or pigs; don't lie to people you love; don't kill anyone who doesn't deserve it.*

There was the problem. Hermana was not entirely sure that Daniel deserved to die. Oh, he deserved to suffer, no doubt. He deserved to get gallstones and gout, and to have a wife who left him and kids who disgraced him. But to die? The more she thought about it, the more Hermana was unsure that anyone deserved to die. It seemed to her that the whole point of punishing someone was to make them sorry. You couldn't be sorry if you were dead.

She stewed in her misgivings as the shadows grew longer outside, and then she recalled the way Ruth's voice had sounded when she'd begged.

Sod him, she thought and ate her eggs.

❋❋❋

The tree branches stretched out like claws to catch Katie as she ran by. She didn't look back, or sideways. She ignored the strange noises, the slitherings in the undergrowth, the high-pitched giggling that seemed to be coming from the tree bark.

She could see the light of Maggie Dim's house in the distance, when two dozen shadows with glowing yellow eyes leapt out onto the path in front of her.

They had been foxes once, she thought. Now they bore a distinct resemblance to the ceramic woodland creatures that sat on the mantelpiece in Mistress's study. Limbs that were too small, heads that were too big, their pelts oddly shiny, their eyes blank and glassy. Beyond that, their ears were shrivelled like dead leaves and their panting mouths were so wide that, looking down into one of them, Katie could see the tip of a tail, a mouse or possibly a rat, poking up from the bottom of its throat.

116

Katie had grown up under the scrutiny of Mistress's ceramics. She despised them. Two of the marks next to Charlie's name in Mistress's little book were there on account of his having touched one of them.

"All right," she said. "All right."

She charged. Four of them came at her, yellow foam trailing from their gaping jaws. They jumped higher than any fox should have been able to jump and landed on her shoulders and chest. To her surprise, they weighed almost nothing; it was as though they were all hollow inside. They snarled and hissed at her, but they had no claws to give them purchase. Pulling them off was more revolting than difficult. Two of them tried to bite her ankles with rotten, black teeth. They couldn't get through her socks, and she slapped them away with her bare hands.

She didn't slow down. They weren't fast, though none of them had skirts to catch on brambles. Maggie's house was so close now, and as she kicked away another horrid fox-thing, she summoned a final burst of speed.

When the doorknob was not ten feet away, she tripped. Whimpering, she scrabbled to her feet and spun around, bracing her back against the door.

There was nothing behind her.

Defying the instinct to knock politely, she slammed her fist onto the door. When no one answered, she kicked it and shouted blue murder with one eye toward the road, fearful that Gregor and his men might appear at any moment.

At last, the door swung open, and Hermana stared down at her. "You? What the hell are you doing here?"

It had been a long week for Katie Bellows.

Poking a finger at Hermana's chest, she hissed, "You're a nasty, spiteful brat, and you think you're better than me because you don't have to work for a living, except you're *not*. You're worse than anyone I've ever met in the village, and I've met the worst. If you don't let me in right this minute, I'm going to *spit* on you."

A gnarled hand appeared on Hermana's shoulder, dragging her out of the way.

"Oh, it's you," said Maggie. "What are you doing here, girl? It's not safe to be out in the woods this late in the day."

"Gregor's coming with a pack of men, Missus Dim. He's been saying that you're to blame for things going bad. I don't think all of them believe him, but a few of them do, and the rest are drunk."

"I see. Hermana! Put the fire out and bring the pig. We're off."

"Quickly!" squeaked Katie. She thought she'd just heard Gregor's voice in the distance.

Hermana emerged bearing a portly swine in her arms. Shutting the door behind her, Maggie said, "We'll go to Ruth's house. Both you girls stay behind me. Don't stop for anything."

She seized Katie's right hand and Hermana's left, and they ran into the darkness.

Chapter Twenty

Daniel had lost his hat.

"We do not have time for this!" Ruth screamed.

"Patience, patience," he said as he searched the surrounding foliage. He stepped carefully to avoid the withered leaves littering the ground, several of which were running about on centipede-like legs.

Ruth clutched her head in despair. It had been going so well. He'd been ready at the appointed time and didn't seem to be having any second thoughts. If anything, he seemed excited, chattering amicably as she led him up to the mushroom patch. Then he'd noticed that his hat was missing.

"It must have snagged on a branch somewhere around here," he said, peering up into the canopy.

"Daniel, I'll buy you a new one," she pleaded.

He laughed. "Ruth, bless you. That hat cost more than your house. Give me a moment... Ah-hah!"

The yellow-spotted branch that had seized the hat was twisted into the shape of an eagle's claw. It held the troublesome piece of haberdashery fifteen feet over their heads.

"Rats," said Daniel, stepping up to the trunk. "Never mind, this will only take a moment. I'm good at this—I used to climb up my cousin Jean's ivy—"

"I'll do it," Ruth interrupted, pushing him aside. She would have been the faster climber even if Daniel hadn't been encumbered by his cape, his heavy boots and gloves, and his scabbard. Either way, the last thing she needed was for the fool to fall off and break his neck before she could stuff the heart down it.

The tree's trunk was soft and warm. It squelched beneath her hands as she climbed. Knots in the wood opened up, revealing white orbs which blinked at her.

"You're doing well!" called Daniel. She realised that he could see straight up her skirt, and rolled her eyes.

When she came within reach of the hat, the tree made a sound like water being sucked down a hole. Ten green shoots grew from the underside of the branch she was clinging to. Within seconds, the shoots were twigs, then thin branches. By the time Ruth's fingers closed around the hat all ten were as wide as her arm and their ends had grown into sharp claws, which tried to grab at her. Snarling, Ruth took out the goblin's knife and swung wildly at them. She found that they were as soft as the rest of the blighted tree, and cutting them back was easy.

"To the devil with you," she spat, clutching the hat to her chest and preparing to climb down.

"I say, what's this?"

Ruth looked down. At the bottom of the tree, a flower had sprouted. It had a tall stem and huge, garishly pink petals. Daniel stood before it, stroking his chin as though he were enjoying a day at the zoo.

"What an extraordinary specimen," he said. "I wonder if Father would like it for his collection of oddities?"

"Get away from it!" she shouted, climbing down as fast as she could. "What are you— AARGH!"

A lump of something black and glistening had been spat out of the pink petals, landing right across Daniel's eyes. He reared back, clawing at his face. "I can't see! I can't see! Oh God, it stings!"

"Calm down, I'm coming!"

From where she was, she couldn't clearly see what happened next. It looked as though the flower darted forward and bit Daniel's arm. He gave an agonised yell, then turned, and ran.

Cursing, Ruth jumped the final two metres, breaking the flower's stem with her landing and stomping on its petals for good measure. Dropping the hat, she chased after him. "*Daniel!*"

She would have caught up with him, had he not run blindly into a wide puddle of the yellow filth. As soon as he stepped in it, it opened up beneath him like quicksand, or like the tiger trap Ruth and Hermana had once dug before learning that the woods did not have any tigers. In the blink of an eye, it swallowed him up.

"Daniel! Daniel?"

She didn't dare dive in after him. She found a long stick and lowered it in, but no matter how hard she stirred it around, nothing rose to the top; not Daniel, not even bubbles. Dropping it, she screamed with rage and frustration until her throat hurt, and then she took off running in the direction of the mushroom patch.

Chapter Twenty-One

As soon as Katie and her grandmother were safely ensconced in Ruth's house, Hermana slipped out the back door. Running into the woods, she saw a bright orange glow in the distance and thought, *They're burning my house.*

Setting her jaw, she broke into a run. There would be time to deal with Gregor later.

She was late. Would Ruth and Daniel already be at the mushroom patch? Or would Daniel be trying to weasel his way out of it? Hermana ran faster, trying not to notice the eerie slithering sounds coming from the undergrowth or the dozens of yellow eyes peering out at her from the shadows. Then she came upon the mound.

It was about six feet high, lying right in her path. She couldn't imagine what sort of animal could have made it. Had it been much, much smaller, she'd have guessed a mole.

As she watched it, the mound shook. It shook again and shuddered and then it broke apart, spraying her with earth. From its depths emerged a...thing.

It had about thirty legs that stuck out of its huge, centipede-like body at different angles. It had no lower jaw, and its tongue was as long as Hermana was tall. It had a dozen small, black eyes clustered together in the centre of what might generously be described as its face. It went, "Wuuargh."

That was all the prompting Hermana needed. She ran like hell.

Because she was a wicked woman and because God only existed for village girls and, who knew, perhaps because she hadn't always brushed her teeth when she was small, it chased her, its bloated belly scraping on the ground. It kept up with her despite its bizarre and disproportionate legs, and she could feel its hot breath on her back of her scalp.

123

Then there was a short, wet *thuck* sound.

Hermana kept running, before realising that she could no longer hear it following her. She looked back and found it lying on its side, a spear jutting from its head and the goblin woman standing over it.

"Where the fuck have you been?" Hermana seethed. "Get me to the mushroom patch! Now!"

The goblin pulled her spear free of the monster's skull, then picked up Hermana, threw her over one shoulder, and ran.

※※※

Shortly after Gregor's men had set off, the villagers had seen an oily sea of yellow filth heading down the main road towards the centre of town. No one could tell where it was coming from; it seemed to seep out of the ground. Soon it was spreading across the village square, coating cobblestones and wheelbarrows and anything else in its path. At a glance, it looked not unlike watery porridge, but for its colour. Those who had good eyesight observed that it wasn't simply rolling towards them in the manner of water when the river burst its banks. Instead, it was inching forward like a giant slug, as though some huge muscle beneath it were contracting in waves.

They put down bags of earth and sawdust in an attempt to block its path. It slithered right over them. When it reached their doors, it dissolved them and began trickling into their houses. Soon the villagers found that there were few places left for them or their livestock to stand. Several unfortunate cattle didn't move out of its way fast enough and their bodies were seen writhing and contorting into hideous shapes before they were submerged.

"Bring ladders!" Joan shouted. "We need to get onto the rooftops!"

As ladders were brought out, the villagers pressed closer and closer together, small children clambering up onto the shoulders of adults. Joan hoisted up Charlie Bellows and wondered if she'd ever see his sister again.

When Maggie saw that Hermana had snuck away, she sighed.

"I could go looking for her," said Katie, meekly.

"No. There's no point both of you being in danger. Besides, I hear singing. Gregor's on his way."

The two of them looked out the window and saw the mob approaching down the road, lit by an orange glow.

"Missus Dim, let's make a run for it. We could go down to the village. I could hide you in the stables until they've calmed down."

"You're a kind girl, Katie Bellows. On balance, though, I think I'd rather have this put to rights now."

A few moments later, there was a loud knock on the door.

As Maggie stepped outside, she took note of their faces. She recognised several of them, anxious fathers and husbands who had knocked on her door in the dead of night months or years or decades ago, entreating her to hurry down to the village with them and save a loved one's life—telling her she was their last hope, now that the physic and the priest had failed.

Ungrateful bastards.

"Good evening, Missus Dim," Gregor said.

"Evening," she said.

"Could you step outside a moment, please? We'd like to have a word."

Then Gregor's brow furrowed. "Katie? That you?"

Standing at Maggie's shoulder, Katie's voice quavered. "Good evening, Mister Markbridge."

"What you doing here, Kates? It's not safe. Come over to me, darling. I'll get one of my boys to take you home."

Katie looked out on a sea of toothy leers. Balling her fists in her dress, she replied, "Mister Markbridge, I think you should leave Missus Dim alone."

"'Leave her alone'? That makes it sound like we were going to do something horrible. Katie, Katie— You know we're not bad men. We're here representing the village. We've got questions for Missus Dim, straightforward and legitimate questions. Asking questions isn't a crime, is it? It's not our fault if she doesn't want to cooperate. Missus

Dim, I'll ask again; will you kindly step outside?"

"No. Piss off."

Amidst the many unsettling and uncanny noises issuing forth from the infected trees surrounding the house, there came what sounded like a giggle. Gregor jumped and then scowled. "Right, bugger this. Let's get them both out here."

✷✷✷

As the last of the villagers climbed up the ladders to safety, the rest sat on the roofs of their houses and shops, watching as the village was submerged beneath the filthy tide. It was up to the windowsills now, and rising at a steady pace.

Joan, Sam, and Charlie had taken refuge atop the mayor's house, along with a dozen other adults and eight children. There wasn't much room, and there were still five people making their way up the ladders. Chickens and goats were being pushed over the side to make space.

"Father," said Joan to the priest, her voice hoarse from shouting. "Perhaps you would like to lead us in prayer?"

"Not really," said the priest, clasping his elderly cat to his chest. Someone had made the suggestion that she go the way of the chickens. "Can't be arsed. Does anyone have any brandy?"

"Sheriff!" came a sharp voice. "Sheriff!"

Lady Piper sat on the edge of the roof, her voluminous skirts taking up twice as much space as her body.

"How can I help you, ma'am?" said Joan, stepping over a sheep and two children.

Lady Piper beckoned her closer and then said into her ear, "Sheriff, you're an intelligent woman. You must have noticed that there is limited space on this rooftop. Once those men who are currently on the ladders are up here with us, there will be no room to move. The slightest amount of jostling might send any one of us plummeting off the edge. In the interests of the greater good, I would like to make a suggestion. The roof of the baker's house is very close, and there are far fewer people on it. If we were to pick up two or three of the scrawnier children—young Charlie, for example—we might fling them across the gap to safety. That

126

would give us all more room."

"Lady Piper, the baker's rooftop is a good ten metres distance from our rooftop."

"Yes, well, you've got strong arms. You might manage it. Someone needs to do *something*, Bailey."

Joan stared down at the filth in silent contemplation. "Lady Piper, do you know where Katie is?"

"Katie Bellows? No, no idea. I suspect the cowardly girl's made a run for it. Shameful, if you ask me. Abandoning an old woman like myself at a time like this. Girls today have no sense of honour or loyalty. If I ever see her face again, I'll discipline the daylights out of her."

Joan looked from the filth to Lady Piper and then back again.

✳✳✳

A little way from the mushroom patch, there was an old apple tree. Its gnarled boughs were weighted down by dozens of objects that resembled apples at a distance. A closer look revealed them to be tiny green heads, childlike and with pips for eyes. They were singing tunelessly in thin, high voices.

Hermana and the goblin were both staring at it as they passed, and both failed to see Ruth running in the other direction until she'd collided with them.

"Where's Daniel?" was the first thing Hermana said when they had picked themselves up.

"Daniel's not coming," Ruth said, shortly.

"What? Ruth, we need him. The whole plan—"

"He's not coming. I'm going to eat it. You go home."

Hermana's brow furrowed. "What... You...but it's dangerous. Remember? We don't know if the heart's poisonous or not."

"Do you have a better plan, Dim?" Ruth demanded and then sniffed the air. "What's that smell? Something's burning."

"Gregor set fire to our house. Don't worry—Gran's all right," Hermana said. She gazed into the slithering shadows behind the trees, hoping Daniel might yet emerge.

"Pigs," muttered Ruth. "They'd deserve it if we let 'em all die."

127

She started walking up the slope, stopping when Hermana followed her. "Didn't you hear me? *I'm* going to eat it. You fuck off back home and check on your gran."

"Don't be thick. I'm not going to go prancing home to sit on my arse while you stay up here eating poison."

"We don't know for a fact that it's poisonous. And if it is, you think I want you there with me blubbering while I twitch my last? Go home, Hermie."

"We'll halve it," said Hermana. "That way, if it *is* poison, we'll only get a half dose each. All right? Good, glad we agree."

"We *don't* agree! Hermie!" shouted Ruth as Hermana started to march up to the patch.

❋❋❋

An hour ago, Gregor had had a clever idea.

As he and his mates had started to make their way up the slope towards Maggie Dim's house, it had occurred to him that it might well be dangerous to wander around a cursed forest after dark. Scratching his head, he'd remembered an old legend his mother had taught him.

"Listen," he'd said to the others. "I want one of you to run to Lady Piper's house and steal some salt from her pantry."

"Why?" his brother had asked him.

"Salt keeps evil spirits away, Phillip. Mum always said so. We're going up against a witch in a forest that's been taken over by black magic. Best be on the safe side."

"He's right," said one of the others. "I spoke to a couple of the servants working up at the chalets. They said that the fancy folk were putting down salt to protect themselves."

Gregor's brother had sprinted to Lady Piper's mansion and returned carrying a jar full of salt. There was just enough of it for every one of them to sprinkle some on his pitchfork and on his palms.

A very clever idea, Gregor thought, mentally patting himself on the back as he strode towards Maggie Dim. The salt clinging to his palms gave him the confidence to seize hold of the old witch's arm without fear of any repercussions.

A second later, the arm he was holding turned green, and Gregor Markbridge got the worst fright of his life.

Chapter Twenty-Two

As Maggie's disguise slipped away, Gregor let go of her arm and took a step back, his mouth agape. The rest of them were frozen, too frightened to move.

"Oh, damn," she muttered.

It didn't take long for the green tinge to spread up Maggie's arm and then across her face. Her hair grew longer, bursting out of its bun, and she felt her mouth fill with sharp teeth. Her human bones creaked as they changed, becoming harder than diamond. Gregor seemed to shrink before her eyes, until she realised that she was getting taller.

Recovering himself, Gregor seized the nearest torch and waved it at her. "You see, boys? I was right!"

Any reservations the villagers may have had about burning an old woman alive vanished. Those who were not scared out of their wits held up their torches and pitchforks and charged.

From out of the ground, bright green vines erupted and twined around their ankles, evoking yelps and howls of pain as they tightened. The villagers' weapons clattered to the ground as they tried in vain to free themselves.

"Curse you, woman!" Gregor bellowed. "How are you doing this?"

"I'm not," Maggie said. "The forest's my home, Mister Markbridge. It's protected me from your sort for years."

She was now two heads taller than Gregor, around whose arms and neck the vines had wrapped themselves. Taking hold of his beard, she said, "You know, boy, back in the good old days we used to eat men like you. We didn't need to. We had other things to eat. We did it for *fun*."

Beneath her feet, red and purple flowers were blooming. As the vines grew tighter and the tighter the air became painfully hot, and the bushiest moustaches began to singe as the screams of the mob rose in pitch. Blisters appeared across Gregor's face.

Maggie smiled. "Now let me see... What shall we do with..."

Then her nose twitched. Her sense of smell was better than any mortal creature's, but while she'd been in her disguise all her senses had been as weak as a human's.

I know that scent, she thought, gazing up the mountain slope.

To herself, she murmured, "How did that happen? Why would the stupid bugger choose to die *here*? This world's supposed to be off-limits."

"Let me go, witch," Gregor hissed.

The sound his neck snapping rang out like a gunshot.

"Do what you want with the rest, Miss Bellows," Maggie said to Katie, before starting to run towards the trees.

Agog at Gregor's dangling corpse, Katie retained enough presence of mind to shout, "I don't understand! What should I..."

"They're all yours," Maggie called back over her shoulder. She was moving faster than any old woman Katie had ever seen; faster than any human. "Do with them as you see fit."

As Maggie disappeared into the woods, the remaining men turned to Katie.

"Katie-girl? Help us get these vines off, there's a love," Gregor's brother begged.

She didn't hear him. She'd already gone back inside, to see if there might be a kitchen knife lying about.

✳✳✳

They spent ages arguing. Eventually, Ruth gave in. One of the reasons they were one another's favourite people was because both of them respected the other's right to make their own frothingly stupid decisions.

"When I was a kid, I used to plan my funeral," said Ruth as they walked up to the mushroom patch. "I spent ages working out the details. What my coffin would look like, where I'd be buried, what songs I'd want people to sing. And now I might be about to die without even leaving behind a bloody will. Doesn't seem fair."

"Don't be thick. Who would you have made a will for?" said Hermana, trying to lighten the mood. "All you've got are your clothes and the dead bug collection in the box under your bed, and you always said I could have those if you ever popped your clogs."

For no real reason, Ruth grinned. "Yeah, I suppose I did."

There was a great deal Hermana wanted to say. But the words that rose in her throat were too small, and if they *were* about to die she didn't want the last things she ever said to Ruth to be inadequate.

"Wish I'd said goodbye to Gran," she muttered.

"Wish I'd said goodbye to Ned," said Ruth.

"Wish I'd tasted brandy."

"Wish I'd been to the city."

"Wish we'd been to the sea."

"Wish it'd been you."

"What're you talking about?"

"What d'you think, you stupid bitch? My last kiss. I wish it hadn't been fucking Daniel. I wanted it to be you."

Hermana stopped walking. Bending down, she pressed her finger into the contaminated soil—reminding herself to clean her hands later on the off-chance that they survived this—and traced four large capital letters. "See that? That spells 'Ruth'. That was the first word I learned how to write. I made Gran teach me how to spell it properly before any of the others."

Ruth leant in close so their noses touched. "If we don't die, promise to show me how to write your name."

"All right. Promise."

The goblin woman followed behind them in silence as they climbed over the Cod. Remembering how bad the mushroom patch had been last time, Hermana braced herself. She half expected to see the trees walking around like people, or that the corpse had come back to life and was waiting for them with a knife.

The one thing she didn't expect to find was Maggie.

Chapter Twenty-Three

At least there wasn't any blood.

Actually, that might have made it better. Blood was normal. Hermana understood blood. The corpse's chest, though it had been cut open, was dry as a bone. There was nothing to obscure her view of its insides, its four lungs and its ribcage that seemed to be made of diamond.

Her grandmother crouched over it, the heart in her hands. She looked up at them and Hermana saw that her mouth was full, her cheeks bulging.

"Gran?" she said, or whimpered. Was this another of the corpse's tricks? A monster made to look like her grandmother?

Maggie finished chewing and swallowed. "Girls, what are you doing up here? And who's that with you?"

The goblin woman started talking. Even though Hermana couldn't understand her words, they sounded accusatory, almost enraged.

Maggie frowned at her and replied, "As you ask, I'm the person who owns these woods. The woods your fool of a husband decided to die in."

Running her eyes from Maggie's feet to her pointed ears, the goblin spoke again, this time in derisive tones.

"Yes, I have gotten older. I like ageing. It's good for you," Maggie said curtly, and took another bite out of the heart.

"Gran, don't!" Hermana cried. "It's poisonous, it's..."

"No, it's not," said Maggie, swallowing. "Not to me, at any rate. What gave you that idea?"

Bewildered, Hermana gestured weakly towards the goblin. "She...she wouldn't eat it herself. She wanted me and Ruth to do it. So we thought..."

"Clever girl," said Maggie. "That was a sensible inference, even if it was completely wrong. No, she didn't want to do it herself because our custom dictates that wives can't perform the funeral ritual."

"'Our custom'? Gran, what are you talking about?"

"Sorry to interrupt," said Ruth, her voice high and thin. "Just wanted to check that I've not gone mad. Hermie, that is your grandmother, yes? And she is…"

"Green, yeah, I noticed that."

"Girls, I'll explain everything if you give me a moment." Maggie stuffed the last lump of heart into her mouth, chewed, and swallowed it.

Hermana and Ruth watched, clutching one another, as the corpse's indestructible flesh melted, dripping down its face and sides until only a bone white skeleton remained. Then that felt to pieces, and the pieces turned to dust.

❋❋❋

A strange wind came down from the mountain, blowing away the smell. Past all hope of reprieve, the villagers clustered together on their rooftops and wondered what fresh hell was at hand.

As they watched, the sea of filth stopped advancing. The many-headed rodents and mutated livestock all fell dead. Those among the villagers who were afflicted with the spots yelped and shouted to see them fade away, leaving faint pink scars in their place.

"We're saved," said Joan, as the priest whooped loudly and kissed his cat.

Later, to Joan's relief, as they climbed down from the rooftops onto the hardened bed of filth, no one asked where Lady Piper had gone.

❋❋❋

As soon as the body disappeared, the goblin woman fell to her knees wailing and clutching her hair.

"Oh, stop it," said Maggie, getting to her feet. "You should have sorted this out weeks ago. People have died because you didn't want to break with tradition. More's the point, you endangered *my* family. We'll be having words about that later, I can assure you."

136

She turned to the girls, the greenness seeping from her skin as she summoned up her human disguise again. "I suppose you'll be wanting an explanation now, my dears?"

Wordless, they both nodded. Maggie sighed. "All right, then. Let's go home."

Chapter Twenty-Four

The next day, Katie stood before the mansion with Charlie clutching at her skirt.

As the filth had hardened, it had taken on the texture of charcoal. Those who were not busy searching for missing family members were scraping it off walls and windows and raking it into a great mound in the town square. Others were running to and from the mound with wheelbarrows, carrying it load by load to a pit being dug in one of the burned fields.

Like most every other remaining structure in town, the mansion was a wreck. The rose bed had been decimated, the ornamental trees were leafless and dying, and the ivy that had arched over the front door had been reduced to a few brown stems. Stranger was the sense of deep quiet that emanated from the hall as Katie stepped in through the servants' door, her ears craning for the daily bustle and fuss entailed in the maintenance of her ladyship's home.

She found no one in the kitchen, nor in the servants' quarters. She went upstairs and found that the whole house was empty. Mistress's bedroom and study had been looted, stripped of linen and silverware, and several dozen books were missing. Her Book of Little Problems had been judiciously cut into pieces and left to marinade in the chamber pot.

She came upon Freddie sitting at the bottom of the main staircase, his hands in his lap and a bottle of Mistress's best brandy at his side.

"Did we have a war while I was out?" she asked.

"Oh, you're alive. That's nice. We all thought you'd gone the way of her ladyship."

"Her ladyship?"

"She's dead. Fell off the roof. I saw the muck swallow her up."

Charlie clapped his hands, adopting an appropriately sombre

expression when his sister glared at him.

"So what do we do now?" Katie asked.

Freddie scratched his head. "Well, the sheriff's deputy's gone missing too, they say. I thought I might apply to be his replacement. As for you... I suppose you can do what you like."

Katie sat beside him for an hour or so, thinking. Then she packed her bags and departed, taking with her a pair of Lady Piper's softest slippers.

"Miss Bellows!" cried the sheriff half an hour later when she opened her front door. Her eyes were red and puffy. Hiding behind her leg, little Sam peered anxiously up at Katie. "Thank God you're all right! I looked everywhere for you, I thought that..."

"Joan, I've lost my job, and I've nowhere to go. I thought I might see if you wanted a maid. I can polish, turn down a bed, dust, sweep, make tea, wash windows, sew, knit, and cook a simple meal. I know you don't earn a great deal of money; for now, I'll be happy if you'd just let me and Charlie stay in your house and eat at your table."

How dreadfully forward she was being, she thought. Murdering several men with a big knife did wonders for one's self-confidence.

Joan blanched, blushed, and succumbed to babbling. "Katie, I don't know what to say. Do you really think you could be happy in my house? It's small, you know. Nothing like Lady Piper's. And well, it's not terribly clean. I think there's a mouse problem, and..."

As she prattled on, Katie placed a hand on her shoulder and manoeuvred her to one side, ushering Charlie into the house. He and Sam regarded one another curiously before Sam, with a serious air, took his hand and lead him over to a corner of the living room where there lay a toy train and a tower of colourful bricks.

"...and when it rains we get leaks, horrible leaks, and there's a dodgy floorboard that I've been meaning to get to and..."

"Sheriff, why don't we have some tea?"

Chapter Twenty-Five

"Go on, try one more time," said Ruth.

Hermana concentrated, pressing the heel of her bare foot into the soil once again. After a moment, a tiny green shoot sprung up next to it.

"Oh my God! You did it!" Ruth squealed, dropping to her hands and knees to inspect Hermana's creation.

"Come off it; it's not that impressive," said Hermana. "Orelzeia can make dozens of them sprout up without even thinking about it."

Hermana still couldn't pronounce the goblin woman's name properly. Since the corpse had disappeared she'd hung around the woods, spending a good deal of time skulking outside Hermana's house. Most of the time she would ignore them. Every now and then, though, she would seize Hermana and drag her into the woods to try to teach her something: how to make flowers grow or how to wield her massive spear or how to talk to squirrels. Hermana didn't have much skill or, to be honest, much interest in any of those things, but she'd kept trying with the flowers because Ruth thought it was cool.

"You're mostly human. Of course it's going to be more difficult for you. Besides, I think it's a good thing that you've got to put some effort into it. Think of how much harder life would be if you left flowers everywhere without even noticing."

She's got a point. Maggie had told them that keeping the flowers from popping up everywhere she walked had been one of the greatest challenges she'd faced when she'd run away from the world she'd been born in and had tried to pass for a human. It had taken her decades to get it under control, in which time she'd married a handsome human and watched him die, then had a daughter, then a granddaughter.

"I always meant to go back home one day," she'd said to Hermana. "But I couldn't leave your mother, and she wouldn't leave these woods."

Hermana hadn't found time to put forward more than a third of the thousands of questions she had. There was so much to be done. Gregor's corpse had to be disposed of; the animals had to be cared for; the vegetable patch had to be set right. That was their task for this morning, Ruth having had the mad idea that Hermana could use her magic goblin feet to grow carrots and cabbages. So far, it hadn't worked.

Thankfully, they weren't in danger of starving. They'd visited the chalets earlier that morning, finding that their residents had all fled as soon as the filth had begun to creep in through their windows. They'd raided their larders and made off with enough coin to buy the moon.

Daniel hadn't turned up yet.

"Poor lad," Hermana had said when Ruth had shown her the spot where he'd disappeared. It now looked like any other part of the woods. There wasn't even any blood.

"You couldn't care less, could you?" Ruth had said.

"Not really."

Gazing down at the small green shoot now, Hermana felt another of those odd pangs of guilt over how little guilt she felt for being complicit in Daniel's disappearance.

"Wipe that mopey look off your face," Ruth said. "I told you it wasn't your fault."

"You know, Ruthie, you'd have been a noblewoman if you'd married him. Hell, he was thirty-something in line for the throne. You could've been a queen if you'd played your cards right. Could've had a crown and a palace all your own."

"What would I have done with a stuffy old palace, hmm? I'd get bored of it in a week." Cracking a smile, Ruth added, "I wouldn't have minded a crown, though."

Concentrating hard, Hermana pressed her thumb into the earth. A second green shoot emerged. It grew straight up until it was two inches tall, then its stem turned left and grew sideways, making a circle. It looped once, twice, three times, and little yellow-white buds popped out all over it.

"Hah! Wasn't sure I could do that," Hermana said, picking up the crown of honeysuckle and handing it to Ruth.

"Show-off," said Ruth as she put it on her head.

"Jealous bitch," said Hermana, and she kissed her.

✸✸✸

Lady Piper's funeral had taken place the previous evening, and the last piles of dead vermin and livestock had been burned. Now the sheriff and her deputies were spread throughout the decimated fields, scouring the ground for any remaining corpses. In addition to the forty-six confirmed deaths, there were still a dozen or so men who remained unaccounted for.

Walking at Joan's side, Katie wondered if she would ever tell her about the three hours she had spent helping Maggie Dim dig a deep hole in the shade behind Ruth's house.

"It's going to be a hard winter," said Joan gloomily, surveying the devastation surrounding them. "We might have to consider moving to... Who on earth is that?"

Katie followed her gaze. To her astonishment, she saw a naked green woman standing at the edge of the field.

As Katie and Joan watched, the bizarre stranger strode through the withered stalks until she reached the exact centre of the field. Once there, she made an odd gesture with her hands.

Rows upon rows of wheat and barley shot up, fully grown and flourishing, as though a giant fist had punched them out of the earth. Katie and Joan instantly lost sight of the deputies and the village, though they could clearly hear the cheers and prayers of thanks that arose a few moments later.

"We're all right," said Joan. "We're going to be all right."

Katie laughed giddily as the sheriff picked her up and swung her around, the wind blowing off her bonnet and letting sunlight dance through her hair.

Epilogue

Daniel didn't know where he was. The sky was red and all the trees were absurdly large. It was night, but there didn't seem to be any stars in the sky, only two giant moons.

After spending several hours wandering aimlessly around, trying to work out what the hell had happened, he finally ran into a group of hunters. They were wearing green body paint, and all of their ears had been mutilated so that they ended in points.

Some strange foreign custom, no doubt, he thought.

His hopes of asking them for directions were dashed when it turned out that he couldn't understand a word they were saying. He tried to explain his position using gestures and received only blank looks in return. Their leader, who carried a very big spear, quickly seemed to lose her patience. She exchanged a few words with the others before all of them started to walk away.

"I say! Don't go!" Daniel called. With nothing better to do, he followed them.

In another world, in a quiet wood, a badger was lining its burrow with the shreds of a fine hat.

About the Author

T.J. Land is a South African writer of erotic romance and sometimes other things. She reads a lot of early modern plays and watches a lot of cartoons. She's going to marry Mrs Lovett when she grows up, although she doesn't expect that to happen for a while.

SunFire Press Imprint

NineStar Press, LLC

www.ninestarpress.com